Rave Reviews for
FRANCIS RAY

Forever Yours

"*Forever Yours* is funny, touching, spicy, and delightful."	—Ann Maxwell

"A wonderfully warm and witty tale with just the right blend of sassiness and tenderness."

—Dorothy Garlock

"A delightful romp down the road of romance."
—Sandra Canfield

One Night with You

"Tenderness and passion that smolder between the pages."	—*Romantic Times BOOKreviews*

Nobody But You

"Fast and fun and full of emotional thrills and sexy chills. Everything a racing romance should be!"
—Roxanne St. Claire

Until There Was You

"Ms. Ray has given us a great novel again. Did we expect anything less than the best?"
—*Romantic Times BOOKreviews* (4 stars)

"Crisp style, realistic dialogue, likable characters, and [a] fast pace."	—*Library Journal*

MORE...

The Way You Love Me

"A romance that will have readers speed-reading to the next tension-filled scene, if not the climax."

—Fresh Fiction

"Fans of Ray's Grayson and Falcon families will be thrilled with the first installment in the new Grayson Friends series. And this is done very well…told with such grace and affection that this novel is a treat to read." *—Romantic Times BOOKreviews* (4 stars)

"Francis Ray is, without a doubt, one of the Queens of Romance." *—Romance Review*

Only You

"Francis Ray's graceful writing style and realistically complex characters give her latest contemporary romance its extraordinary emotional richness and depth." *—Chicago Tribune*

"It's a joy to read this always fresh and exciting saga." *—Romantic Times BOOKreviews* (4 stars)

"The powerful descriptive powers of Francis Ray allow the reader to step into the story and become an active part of the surrender…If you love a great love story, *Only You* should be on your list."

—Fallen Angel Reviews

"Riveting emotion and charismatic scenes that made this book captivating…a beautiful story of love and romance."   —*Night Owl Romance*

"A beautiful love story as only Francis Ray can tell it."
                    —Singletitles.com

"A warm and wonderful contemporary romance with plenty of humor and drama. Adding a fun warmth and reality to these characters and a plot that moves quickly add all the needed incentive to read this fun book."   —*Multicultural Romance Writers*

Irresistible You
"Another winner…witty and charming…Francis Ray has a true gift for drawing the readers in and never letting them go."   —*Multicultural Romance Writers*

Dreaming of You
"A great read from beginning to end."
                    —*Romantic Times BOOKreviews*

"An immensely likable heroine, a sexy man with a heart of gold, and touches of glitz and color, [this] is as unapologetically escapist as Cinderella. Lots of fun."   —*BookPage*

You and No Other

"The warmth and sincerity of the Graysons bring another book to life....delightfully realistic."

—*Romantic Times*

"Astonishing...the best romance of the new year...the Graysons are sure to leave a smile on your face and a longing in your heart for their next story."

—RomanceReview.com

"Great love stories." —*Booklist*

Someone to Love Me

"Another great romance novel." —*Booklist*

"The plot moves quickly, and the characters are interesting." —*Romantic Times*

"The characters give as good as they get, and their romance is very believable." —*All About Romance*

Forever Yours

Francis Ray

St. Martin's Paperbacks

This is a work of fiction. All of the characters, organizations, and events portrayed in this novel are either products of the author's imagination or are used fictitiously.

FOREVER YOURS

Copyright © 1994 by Francis Ray.
Excerpt from *It Had To Be You* copyright © 2010 by Francis Ray.

Cover photograph © Shirley Green

For information address St. Martin's Press, 175 Fifth Avenue, New York, NY 10010.

ISBN: 978-0-312-36508-0

Printed in the United States of America

PINNACLE BOOKS edition / July 1994
St. Martin's Paperbacks edition / April 2010

St. Martin's Paperbacks are published by St. Martin's Press, 175 Fifth Avenue, New York, NY 10010.

10 9 8 7 6 5 4 3 2 1

For daddy, Mc Radford Sr, for all the usual reasons and so much more. I couldn't have made it without you.

—K.

Special thanks to Laree Bryant and June Harvey for their invaluable assistance, to Cleo L. Hearn who introduced me to the extraordinary African-American men and women who follow the rodeo circuit, and to my mother, Verona Radford, who instilled in me a love of reading.

Chapter 1

"Have you chosen which one of your young gentlemen you're going to marry, Victoria?"

Stunned, Victoria Chandler stared over the silver tea service at her grandmother. Heart pounding in her chest, Victoria carefully set the clinking cup and saucer on the antique clawfoot cocktail table in front of her. From out of nowhere came the childhood chant "liar, liar, pants on fire". "I . . . er . . . no. I'm still trying to decide."

Clair Chandler Benson's nut-brown face creased into an indulgent smile. "You told me you were having trouble choosing from your four young men. It's a dilemma not many women are faced with. But you've been blessed with the same striking looks as your great-grandmother. Like you, she had long black hair, hazel eyes, and honey-colored skin, a vision. However, I have complete faith your heart will guide you in the twenty-one days you have left."

Feeling as if the floor shifted beneath her feet, Victoria fought the panic that threatened to overwhelm her. "Grandmother, why don't I wait and decide at the end of summer, when things aren't so hectic at the stores?"

Clair shook her blue-gray head of hair. "That won't do at all. It will be beyond the cutoff date and you'll lose *Lavender and Lace*."

Victoria's tenuous hold on her emotions slipped. Fear widened her eyes and left her momentarily speechless. "You-you're serious, aren't you?"

"I've never been more serious about anything in my entire life," Clair answered. "I know we haven't discussed it in some time, but I thought I had made myself quite clear. I remember our agreement well. We were sitting in this very room and I gave you six months to get married or I would call in the loans for your three stores. Victoria, you did mark your calendar, didn't you?"

Slowly Victoria rose to her feet. Her eccentric grandmother wasn't playing. She meant every word. Fool that Victoria was, she thought she could evade the issue by telling her grandmother that she couldn't choose between four men. The trouble was, there were *no* men in her life—and that was the way Victoria wanted to keep it.

"Grandmother, marriage is a serious matter."

"Of course it is. You're talking to someone who celebrated her thirty-fifth wedding anniversary last month." Clair smiled, showing natural white teeth. "I completely understand your apprehension. After my first husband died I never dreamed I'd find anyone like him. Then I met Henry at a charity dinner. I'm sure you'll be as fortunate as I was in finding a wonderful second husband."

"Men have changed since then. They aren't all honest and forthright like grandfather," Victoria said with a tinge of anger.

"I know that, dear, but you've picked the best Fort Worth has to offer; a doctor, a lawyer, a cattleman, and a banker." Clair looked at her only grandchild with unabashed pride. "Although, I must admit I rather favor the cattleman, since you mentioned his ranch is in the area. It would be nice to have a horseman in the family again. Your great-great-grandfather, Hosea Chandler, was a buffalo soldier with the Ninth Cavalry unit."

Victoria groaned inwardly. Those nursery rhymes again. Doctor, lawyer, Indian chief. At the time, she knew even her unconventional grandmother wouldn't have believed Victoria was dating an Indian chief. Out of nowhere a "butcher" and a "baker" had popped into her head. Before she knew it they became a cattleman and a banker.

"What if I can't make up my mind?"

"Oh, dear." Distressed, Clair paused in adding a dollop of cream to her specially blended tea. "Then you might have a problem."

"What do you mean?" Victoria's stomach muscles clenched.

"You know how much your grandfather and I love you, and I was afraid I'd lose my nerve and call off the whole thing. On the other hand, you know how much pride I take in a person keeping their word. So, I turned everything over to my lawyer."

Victoria slumped into the nearest chair. "Grandmother, how could you have done this to me?"

"Because I love you. You're thirty years old and still dragging your feet about remarrying and carrying on the Chandler name. I simply decided to help you."

Sheer panic propelled Victoria once again to her feet. She felt trapped as she glanced around the sitting room full of overstuffed furniture, antiques, and heirlooms that had been handed down through five generations of Chandlers. The Chandlers had been a prominent and well-respected family in Texas since reconstruction and each generation coined the name with pride.

She wondered if the hardships her ancestors endured were any greater than hers had been when she was married to a selfish, greedy man who demeaned her and took from her until nothing was left . . . not even her self-respect. The thought of marriage tied her stomach in knots.

Unconsciously, Victoria shook her head. "I need more time."

"You have twenty-one days." Clair picked up her tea and took a sip, then assessed her granddaughter critically. "Perhaps if you bring your young men over, on separate visits of course, your grandfather and I can help you choose one. You're so compassionate, you're probably worried about the three losers, but it can't be helped."

Victoria looked at the seventy-two-year-old woman who sat before her, lovable and cuddly in chiffon and pearls, and wanted to shake her. But experience had taught Victoria that when her grandmother was in one of her stubborn moods, she developed tunnel vision. It was easier trying to reason with a two-year-old child. Still, for Victoria's own sanity, she had to try. "I'm not marrying anyone in twenty-one days."

"You will if you want to keep *Lavender and*

Lace," Clair reminded her, then leaned back on the blue silk couch. "I told you, it's in my lawyer's hands now. I can't change it. And it isn't as if you don't have any prospects. At least you can choose your own man. In the past, women seldom had that luxury."

True fear began to creep up Victoria's spine. "Grandmother, don't do this. You know how much my shops mean to me. If you love me, you'll stop this now."

"It's because I love you that I won't stop. Besides, I have complete confidence that you'll decide within the time left." Clair looked at her granddaughter with steadfast brown eyes. "When your precious father and mother were killed in that tragic boating accident eighteen years ago, you became the daughter I never had. Each night I say a prayer for that man who pulled you to shore safely. Victoria, your father would have wanted me to guide you in this matter. I've only got a few good years left and I want to see you happily settled before I go."

"I *am* happy," Victoria cried.

"You can lie to yourself, but not to me. I see the wistful look in your face when you see a baby or a small child." Clair set the delicate china on the table. "You are a sensitive, caring woman. You want and deserve children of your own."

Her grandmother's perceptiveness caught Victoria off guard. She had tried to forget her dream of children just as she had tried to forget her failure as a wife. Apparently, she was successful at neither. Her shoulders straightened, causing her emerald green wrap dress to tighten across her hips and rise above her knees.

"Many women want children. My wanting them doesn't prove anything," Victoria said, taking a seat beside her grandmother.

A gentle hand caressed Victoria's shoulder-length hair. "It might not, if you didn't also crave what's required in order to *have* children."

Blushing, Victoria stood and walked to the open French doors on the other side of the room. "I don't know what you're talking about."

"Yes, you do." Shrewd eyes swept Victoria's rigid posture. "You stayed with Stephen out of a sense of duty, not love. You've yet to find the man who can kiss you senseless."

"Grandmother!" Victoria whirled, her mouth open in shock.

"Oh, my darling Victoria," her grandmother said, her eyes twinkling mischievously. "Sometimes you're such an innocent. It's going to be a pleasure to watch you fall in love and blossom."

"Where is grandfather?" Victoria asked as she stepped onto the terrace and looked out over the immaculate lawn to the flower gardens beyond. "Perhaps he can talk some sense into you."

"Henry is in the rose garden and he and I are in perfect agreement." Clair folded her hands in her lap. "We both decided the best way to get you to the altar was through *Lavender and Lace*. You wouldn't raise an eyebrow if we threatened to cut you out of our will."

Anger replaced irritation and fear. Victoria stalked back to her grandmother. "I earn my own way, just like I earned *Lavender and Lace*. I slept in the back office to cut expenses, did without, and worked fourteen hours a day to make the first store successful."

Clair was undisturbed. "Against my advice and wishes, but you proved me wrong. I've never been prouder of you."

"Then give me the time to pick my husband," Victoria said, unable to keep the pleading note out of her voice. She'd spent the last eight years regaining her self-respect and her independence; she wasn't about to let a man destroy her again. "Let me choose in my own time."

Her grandmother shook her coiffured head. "You have twenty-one days or the lawyer will call in the loan. I'm thinking about letting DeShannon manage the stores for me. They'll give Henry's niece a reason to get up before noon." Clair took a sip of tea. "Although I don't know what she'll do once she gets to your office. She's as flighty as a hummingbird," she said almost to herself.

Clair picked up a wafer-thin cookie and critically eyed the cherry center. "Hard to believe your grandfather is related to that family," she continued. "Oh well, that's their side of the family. What I intend to do is preserve mine. The Chandler bloodline will continue in you."

Discarding the cookie, Clair picked up her cup of tea and drew in a long, deep breath. "Smell those roses. Your grandfather is working hard to keep them pretty in hopes you'll change your mind about a civil ceremony and get married in the garden. I hate that you won't be a June bride, but you can't have everything. April is a beautiful month to get married."

Clair glanced sideways at the silent Victoria. "Do you think you could manage to get pregnant right away?" The older woman looked wistful. "I don't want to rush you, but we're all getting older. A boy would be nice, but we could name a girl Chandler to carry on the name, or you could hyphenate Chandler with your married name. Which idea do you like best?"

"Why ask me when you obviously have everything planned?" Victoria said tightly. "You probably have my obstetrician all picked out."

Clair looked thoughtful. "I haven't. Perhaps I should begin looking into the matter. The best ones are difficult to get."

Her head pounding, Victoria plopped into an ornate straight-back chair near the terrace window. How could you love someone and want to throttle them at the same time?

Two days later, the anger and frustration Victoria felt about her grandmother's unimaginable proposition hadn't diminished. She sat in one of downtown Fort Worth's most elegant restaurants and couldn't have cared less. Her salad fork pinged against her plate as she speared an olive. "Grandmother, how could you do this to me?" she said absently.

Seated across the restaurant table from Victoria, Bonnie Taylor lifted a perfectly arched brow and slowly smiled. "So that's why you've been so preoccupied during lunch. I thought there was a problem with one of your stores."

"If grandmother has her way, they won't be my stores in nineteen days."

"So, she was serious about her ultimatum?"

"Yes," Victoria said. "My sweet, loving grandmother deliberately badgered me into borrowing money from her to open another store, planning all along to use the loan as leverage to force me to remarry. I could kick myself for thinking she was just being fanciful and that she'd forget all about her plan in a couple of months."

"I take it the old girl proved you wrong."

"In spades. Unwittingly, I helped her scheme by insisting I put up the other two stores as collateral in case something happened to me. If I default on the loan, I'll lose everything."

Bonnie's light brown eyes sparkled as she looked around the posh dining room, with its high crystal chandeliers, breathtaking murals of angelic cherubs in a blue sky, and hovering waiters in white dinner jackets. "Well, you picked the right place to find a husband." She waved a slender hand toward the floor-to-ceiling draped window twenty feet away from them. "The hotel across the street spans three city blocks. There has to be at least two hundred eligible men registered there and probably half that many are prowling the halls in the attached convention center. Minutes from here is the historic stockyards district, where I bet you'll find another hundred men."

Bonnie ignored Victoria's warning look and continued. "If you don't feel like going to all that trouble, there's a man sitting about four tables behind you near the balcony who hasn't taken his eyes off you since you came in. I'll bet—"

"I'll bet he either has one of those smoldering

looks guaranteed to make a woman's knees weak or he's showing a toothy smile that helped an orthodontist put a hefty down payment on a Porsche," Victoria said without looking behind her.

Bonnie smothered a laugh. "I think he was trying to pull off a combination of the two."

"Men! Most of them think all they have to do is show some muscle, be reasonably good looking and a woman will swoon at their feet."

The teasing look vanished from Bonnie's face. "I haven't seen you this steamed in a long time."

"Can you blame me?" Victoria asked, leaning back in her seat. "I've boxed myself in. If I don't find someone to marry, I'll lose *Lavender and Lace*."

Bonnie frowned. "I know you're scared and angry, and you have a right to be, but marriage isn't that bad. I love being married."

"Of course you do. You're married to a man who worships the ground you walk on. My ex-husband only worshiped my bank account," Victoria said bitterly.

"I know Stephen betrayed you, but not all husbands are monsters. Dan is the best thing that ever happened to me." Bonnie's voice softened. "I can't imagine my life without him."

Victoria nodded. "Maybe because he's an architect, he wants to create, not destroy. The best

decision you ever made was getting bids on reno-
vating that old building for your art gallery. I
vividly remember your jaw coming unhinged
when Dan came by to give an estimate. He was
just as taken with you. I think he loves you now
more than he did when you were married five
years ago. Stephen's so-called love for me didn't
last past the honeymoon cruise." She crunched on
a piece of lettuce. "I've been attracting the rejects
ever since."

"Part of that is your fault, Victoria," Bonnie
replied gently as she picked up her wine glass.

Jerking upright in her tapestry upholstered chair,
Victoria stared at Bonnie. Despite being complete
opposites in background and temperament, they
had been best friends since they were in the sixth
grade. They met when Victoria, painfully shy and
lonely, had enrolled in Eastwood Academy after the
death of her parents. The outspoken Bonnie had
looked at the scrawny kid clutching her books,
her eyes wide and frightened, and taken her under
her wing. "My fault?"

Setting the long-stemmed glass aside, Bonnie
explained. "You're beautiful, independent, and successful. That's intimidating enough to a lot of men.
And since your divorce from Stephen, a trifle hard
on a man's ego. Only a fool, a schemer, or a man in
love is going to let you tramp all over him."

Victoria's delicate features hardened. "After the fiasco with my ex-husband, can you blame me?"

"No, I can't, but Stephen has been history for a long time. That is," she paused. "Until last week."

"I can't believe he had the nerve to call me," Victoria snorted. "I hope the sound of the receiver crashing down gave him an earache for a week." She played with her salad. "Yesterday I learned the reason for his sudden interest. He lost another job."

"He certainly made a mess of his life. On the other hand, you've got to get on with yours. I think your grandmother realized your hesitancy and decided to give you a little push."

Victoria's fingertips drummed out an angry beat on the white tablecloth. "But why did it have to be over a cliff?"

Bonnie laughed. "I'm glad to see you haven't lost your sense of humor. Does it also mean you've decided to quit fighting and get married?"

For once Victoria didn't have a quick answer. No matter how she tried to find a way out of the trap her grandmother had set for her, she came up empty. Clair Benson had Victoria's signature on a legal document. The only way she could find a way out was to sign another legal document. A marriage license. Her stomach clenched. Never again had she wanted to give a man any control of her body or of her life.

"Well?" Bonnie prompted.

Victoria looked at her friend waiting for an answer and knew she had only one choice if she wanted to keep her boutiques. Her face settled into determination. "I'll do whatever it takes to save *Lavender and Lace*. Only this time the marriage will be on my terms. Not my grandmother's. Not the man I choose. This time I'll make the rules."

"I don't suppose you're going to make this easy and fall in love in the next nineteen days?"

Victoria's eyes narrowed. "Love has nothing to do with this. It'll be a business arrangement. A simple transaction for which I'm willing to pay."

Bonnie looked as if she wanted to argue, but all she said was, "How long do you plan to stay married?"

"A year, tops. Anything shorter and grandmother can demand payment in full on my loan." Victoria twirled her fork.

Bonnie pushed aside her salad plate. "I hate to bring this up, but how do you plan to keep your grandparents and everyone else from finding out the marriage is a sham?"

"My husband will travel a great deal. His being gone so much will lend credibility to the eventual divorce." Glancing at the lobster chowder the waiter placed in front of her, Victoria picked up her soup spoon. Her appetite had returned.

Deep in thought, Bonnie didn't pay any attention to the lasagna of shrimp, scallop and spinach set before her. Instead she said, "What you need is a man who has enough integrity not to want your money after the divorce, or one who has enough money not to want yours."

"I know," Victoria said. "I want him to quietly disappear when the time is up. Call it pride or whatever, but I don't want it known that the only way I can get a man is to pay for one. Once was enough."

"Then we need to add 'discreet' to his qualifications," Bonnie said.

Victoria put her spoon down. "You might as well add 'kind,' 'sensitive,' and 'caring' while you're at it."

With a secret smile, Bonnie looked at Victoria. "I have your man."

"What!" A wave of silence followed as stylish heads turned toward their table. Victoria ignored them. "Tell me you're not kidding."

Grinning, Bonnie shook her head, her dark, layered hair brushing against her cheeks. "My cousin, Kane Taggart, is thirty-six, single, and has all the qualities you're looking for."

"Kane?" Victoria's dark brows furrowed. "That name sounds familiar."

Bonnie sucked her teeth. "Why, Victoria Chandler. I never thought you'd forget the name of the man you first slept with."

Outrage and indignation swept across Victoria's face. "Stephen is the on—"

Laughter erupted from Bonnie. "I meant 'slept' literally. How could you forget the night you spent at my house, when that violent storm roared across the city around midnight? We had just graduated from high school, and my parents and your grandparents were out of town. We were shaking as much as the trees." Bonnie fingered the stem of her wine glass. "Tornadoes had been sighted in the area and hail was so loud on the roof we had to shout to hear each other. The phone was out and there was a loud pounding at the door just as the lights went out."

Victoria completed the story. "It was Kane. He had driven through high winds and rain to check on us. Your parents called him when they couldn't reach us."

"It's a wonder we didn't knock him down the way we launched ourselves at him," Bonnie laughed. "I don't see how he managed to get out of his raincoat, because neither one of us would let go of him."

Victoria giggled, Bonnie's laughter infectious. "Yet somehow he got us settled in the hall, with pillows, blankets, a flashlight and a small portable radio he had brought. You went to sleep a couple of hours later, but I don't think I dropped off until around dawn. Sometimes we talked, sometimes we just listened to the rain."

A vague memory about that night tugged at Victoria. A deep, soothing voice and the gentleness with which she was held returned to her. Her parents' hugs had been frequent, but quick. Her grandparents patted her on the hand or on the head. Victoria hadn't realized how wonderful and reassuring it would feel to be held until Kane's arms tightened each time her voice quivered or she shivered. Somehow she had never experienced the same sense of well-being in a man's arms. She quickly attributed the reason to youthful embellishment.

"That morning he was gone. I don't think I ever saw him again," Victoria said quietly.

"You must have. He was in and out of my house the entire summer and so were you. But you started dating Johnny Evans around that time and he was all you talked about until you went to college." Bonnie picked up her fork. "Anyway, Kane's in town for a few days and he came by the house last night to say hello. He wasn't there ten minutes before he asked about you."

"Me?"

"You may not remember him, but he definitely remembers you," Bonnie explained. "I detected a lustful gleam in his black eyes when he said your name."

"I don't want lust. I want a business arrangement," Victoria said, her voice tight and final. She owed Kane her gratitude, not her body.

"That's up to you and Kane." Bonnie took a bite of pasta. "Come over to the house tonight around seven and meet him. Dan should be home from work by then."

"I don't know, Bonnie. Do you think he'll agree to my terms?"

"Kane has a big heart for anyone in trouble. Besides, what have you got to lose?"

Knowing what she had to lose right down to the last square footage, Victoria sighed and said, "I'll be there."

At exactly five minutes to seven, Victoria walked up the curved stone steps to Bonnie's home. A wide expanse of glass showcased the rosewood staircase and elegance of the house in the development Dan had helped design. Working together,

Bonnie and Dan had built their dream house. Immediately, Victoria thought of Stephen. He had destroyed her dreams by working for nothing and grabbing with both hands for any and everything, she thought bitterly.

With grim determination, Victoria brought her mind back to the present. Shifting uneasily in her three-inch heels, she took a deep breath, then brushed an unsteady hand over her magenta-colored raw silk jacket and skirt. She had come this far, she couldn't back down now. No matter how repugnant marriage was to her, she couldn't add another failure to her already seemingly long list.

She was the only child of brilliant parents, yet she was an average student. Not once did she get the lead in a play, make the honor roll or the cut for the drill team. She hadn't dared try out for cheerleaders. Her success on the girls' softball team in her senior year hadn't made up for the failures that continued to dog her after graduation from high school. Because she had dropped out of college at the end of her junior year to get married, she had failed to get her business degree from Texas Southern University.

Lavender and Lace was the one and only success in life that she could look upon as totally hers. She would keep it at all cost. Squaring her shoulders as she always did when faced with a problem, she ran a distracted hand through her wind-tossed hair, then rang the door-bell.

Her hand lifted again just as the heavily carved door opened. Her jaw slackened. Standing in front of her was the brawniest man she had ever seen. He had a rugged, dark brown face. Winged brows arched over piercing black eyes edged with thick lashes. A neatly trimmed mustache defined an uncompromising mouth.

Separately, his features weren't noteworthy, but combined, they created an unusual picture of sharp angles and hard planes, as if someone had done the impossible and sculptured his face from a mountain of granite.

His tall, powerful body reinforced her impression of a mountain. At least six feet five, his white-shirted torso lent new meaning to the term "yard-wide chest." Broad shoulders tapered to a surprisingly flat stomach and narrow waist. A hand-tooled belt, with the initials K.T. on the silver buckle, looped through faded jeans that displayed his muscular build with shameless disregard for propriety.

Her drying throat caused her to snap her mouth shut. *Oh, God! How could I have forgotten a man this overwhelmingly masculine and intimidating?*

Chapter 2

"Hello, Tory. It's nice seeing you again."

Victoria blinked. The soft, modulated voice contrasted dramatically with the towering giant standing in front of her. It was as if Mother Nature had tried to make up for the excess in his size by subduing his voice, then making the tone irresistibly hypnotic.

"Please, come on in."

When she didn't move, gentle, almost caressing fingers closed around her silk-covered elbow and drew her inside. Absently, she wondered why she allowed him to continue holding her once she was over the threshold.

"I take a bit of getting used to," he said easily as he guided her past the formal living area toward the den in the back of the house.

"Er . . . I . . . no. You just startled . . . I mean . . ." She stammered, then flushed.

A deep melodious sound floated over her head. She glanced up to see the walking mountain laughing. The sound was as soothing and as alluring as his voice.

He peered down at Victoria with what she thought were the most compelling eyes she had ever seen . . . soul-stirring and midnight black. She shifted under his penetrating stare, annoyed with the tingling sensation in the pit of her stomach.

"Beautiful women can be forgiven almost anything, Tory. Hope you don't mind me calling you Tory. Victoria sounds too formal," he explained easily. "Let's go find Bonnie. Dan's still at the office and she's using us as guinea pigs to test her cooking skills." He waved Victoria toward a teal leather couch.

Automatically, Victoria perched on the edge of the cushion, her gaze on Kane. She was still trying to get her bearings, though he lounged easily against a winged leather chair with one booted foot crossed over the other. There had been no hesitation when he met her, no awkwardness. She had the feeling that there weren't many situations where he felt as overwhelmed as she did at the moment. A man his size probably hadn't faced too many things that intimidated him.

A thunderstorm with wind gusts of sixty miles an hour hadn't stopped him. She wasn't foolish enough to think he'd let her wishes sway him. Stephen had never listened to her opinion and he had been nowhere near Kane's formidable size.

It would take a special kind of man not to use such obvious strength indiscriminately. The man who calmed her fears while the wind howled and the rain slammed against Bonnie's house had been that type of man. Victoria had learned the hard way that people often let you see what they wanted you to see.

"Can you cook?" Kane asked abruptly.

"I . . . why . . . er . . . yes."

A slow, teasing grin lifted his mustache. "Good."

Victoria blinked. His smile revealed the sensual curve of his lower lip. Warmth curled through her. Unconsciously, she leaned forward to study him closer. How could she have thought his mouth was uncompromising? The sudden knowledge of what she felt, what she was doing, raced through her like wildfire, fierce and frightening. She jerked upright in her seat. The last thing she needed was a man who made her remember she was a woman.

Bonnie entered the room, carrying a clear oblong tray. "Hi, Victoria. Let's try these cheese appetizers while you and Kane get reacquainted."

Kane groaned. "You promised to feed me, not tease me with something the size of my thumb."

"Man does not live by bread alone," Bonnie said meaningfully, then winked at Victoria.

Victoria surged to her feet. "Bonnie, we need to talk."

"In a minute," Bonnie said, setting the tray on a glass coffee table. "Let's eat these while they're hot."

"*Now*," Victoria said, unable to keep the panic out of her voice.

Hands braced on her slim hips, Bonnie straightened. "What's so important it can't wait?"

Victoria was unable to keep from glancing at Kane. What she saw didn't reassure her. She had never seen a person so still and watchful. She swallowed. "I'm sure Kane won't mind excusing us."

"No, I wouldn't. But you don't have to take Bonnie into another room to tell her I'm not what you had in mind as marriage material," he said bluntly.

Victoria whirled to face Kane. She realized she hadn't been able to hide the wild desperation in her voice. He returned her look with an unblinking stare.

"But you're exactly what she had in mind!" Bonnie argued, clearly puzzled as she looked from Victoria to Kane.

"Why don't we let her tell us that," Kane said.

The words wouldn't come. Kane might look as if he was carved out of granite, but nearly twelve years ago he had comforted her and asked for nothing in return. Just as he asked nothing of her now except the truth.

It had been a long time since she had met a man who valued honesty so highly. If nothing else, he earned her grudging respect for that. *If* she was crazy enough to be looking for a real husband, the man watching her with the predatory inertness of a cat might have deserved a closer look.

"Are you always so outspoken?" Victoria asked.

Crossing his arms over his chest, his black eyes narrowed as he peered down at her. "I find it saves time and bother."

"Next time, take the time. I wanted to ask Bonnie how much you knew," she improvised, then lifted her chin at his arched brow. "Obviously, that's no longer necessary."

"You need a husband who doesn't want your money, who won't interfere in your business, and one who, when a year is up, will get lost. Did I leave out anything?" Kane asked.

Voiced by him, her words sounded crude and demeaning, but Victoria had been through too much to back down from the unflattering truth.

"As a matter of fact, you did. This marriage will

be a business, not a personal, transaction. We'll see each other exactly twice; once at the wedding ceremony and twelve months later when we sign the divorce papers. My husband will conveniently travel a great deal. I don't want flowers, candy, or whispers of sweet nothings, or anything from the man I marry except his signature on the license."

Kane's posture relaxed but his eyes were no less penetrating. "Was your first marriage that bad, or that good?"

Victoria's nails dug into the soft leather of her clutch handbag. "My previous marriage will not be open for discussion."

"Under ordinary circumstances I might agree, but if I decide to go along with this, you'll be carrying my name for a year and I think that entitles me to know." He glanced at the silent Bonnie. "Why don't you check on something in the kitchen?"

"We haven't decided—" Victoria began, but her friend had already turned to go. Bonnie hesitated, then walked soundlessly from the room.

"Changed your mind again?" Kane asked, his voice flat and emotionless.

Victoria glanced up at him, watching her with his unnerving black eyes, and realized that if she said yes she would be revealing more than she wanted to reveal. "No."

"Then I suggest we get started. Would you like to sit back down?"

"No." Sitting would only make the next few minutes more difficult. Kane had effectively backed her into a corner. Either she proceeded or she walked. Walking was infinitely preferable to telling him the humiliating and embarrassing truth about the events surrounding her marriage.

"Tory, I hope you realize that Bonnie would never have asked me to help if she thought I couldn't be trusted," Kane said, his voice soothing.

Restlessly, she turned toward the double doors in the back of the room, which allowed a view of the rock garden and the swimming pool. "Is this necessary?"

"If you were in my position, wouldn't you want to know?"

Again the voice was soft and gentle, but no less insistent. Years ago the same voice had been the center of her world for a few hours. She might have become callous, but she hadn't stooped to repaying kindness with cruelty. She'd complete the interview with Kane, tell him she'd get back to him, and start looking for someone else.

"My first marriage was also a business transaction, although at the time I didn't know it. Eleven months and a hundred thousand dollars from my trust fund later, I filed for divorce. Stephen got half of the remaining twenty thousand dollars, and I got my freedom."

"Did you love him?"

Something about Kane's voice had her turning toward him. He was within ten feet of her and again his eyes searched her face with an intensity that unnerved her. Stephen had swept her off her feet with his handsome face, easy charm, and polished manners. They had met at a Christmas party and spent every day together until she went back to college after the winter break. She had been flattered when he came to Houston to see her, and proud of the way the other women in her dorm practically drooled over him.

With stars in her eyes, she had accepted his proposal on Valentine's Day. She had thought it so romantic. It was only after she said "I do" that she realized he intended them to live off her money. He quit his job with an advertising firm and started running up her charge accounts. The considerate, loving man she thought was Stephen didn't exist.

In his place stood a cruel, heartless stranger who made no secret that he loved himself and her money more than he could possibly love her. Nothing she did pleased him, and he was quick to point out her imperfections. Unwilling to admit she had failed again, she stayed in a prison of her own making until his betrayal slapped her in the face. Seeing Stephen and another woman in her bed filled her with an almost uncontrollable rage. The graphic scene she had witnessed also gave her the courage to walk away, taking nothing except her tattered pride.

Victoria finally answered the only way she could. "At one time I thought I did."

Kane took a step closer, bringing with him a disturbing heat that increased her uneasiness. "And now?"

"I think of my stupidity in trusting a man who took with no thought of giving in return," she said, unable to keep the bitterness out of her voice. How could she have been so weak and spineless? "No man will ever make a fool of me again."

"Tory, don't judge all men by Stephen." Kane lifted his callused hand toward her cheek. She reflexively drew back and nearly tripped over a chair.

Quickly, she glanced away from Kane's narrowed eyes. "I don't. In fact, I think as little as possible about men."

"What do I get for my signature?"

Victoria's head jerked up, her brows furrowed

as she tried to determine if the suggestive note in his husky voice was real or imagined. "Ten thousand dollars."

"You pay off one husband and plan to buy another one with the same amount of money. Is that your going price for a man?"

"It worked in the past. Besides, I don't expect a man to marry me for nothing." An arched brow on his hard-looking face told her quicker than her brain that she had said too much. "I . . . I mean that—"

"I get the gist of your meaning." He studied her for a long time. "Do you know that every time I come near you, you flinch or turn away?"

She flushed. Her grip on her purse tightened.

"Well, I guess some things aren't meant to be. Good luck and goodbye, Victoria." Whirling on booted heels, Kane strode toward the kitchen. Despite his size, he moved with the strength and grace of a large cat. "Bonnie, get yourself out here."

A grinning Bonnie came rushing from the kitchen, a portable phone in her hand. "I'm talking to Dan. When's the wedding?"

Kane's face might have been carved out of stone for all the emotion he showed. "I decided that I'm not ready to get married." He hugged a frowning Bonnie. "Tell that husband of yours I'll stop by before I leave for home." He headed for the door.

"I'll call you back, Dan." Throwing the phone on a chair, Bonnie advanced on Victoria. "What did you say to him?"

"Nothing." Victoria watched Kane cross the room and retrieve his black Stetson from the hall tree. There was no doubt in her mind that this time she would never forget him, nor the look of censure on his face before he turned to leave.

"Then why is he leaving after telling me he was going to help you? He's the nicest man I know." Bonnie glared at Victoria. "Some people act stupid when they meet Kane, because of his imposing presence and strong will, but I thought you had more sense."

Victoria almost blurted out that she bet those acting stupid were women. Annoyed with her wayward thoughts, she tunneled her hand through her hair. "You heard him. He's the one saying no, and I have to agree with him. If I get married, it will be on my terms. Kane is probably like a runaway bulldozer when he wants something. Nothing is going to stand in his way."

"You're afraid of him," Bonnie cried incredulously.

"I'm not afraid of any man," Victoria shot back.

Bonnie rolled her eyes heavenward. "Oh, come on, Victoria. This is a girlfriend you're talking to. I've seen that wide-eyed look too many times not to know what it means."

"Kane is not the man for me," Victoria cried stubbornly.

"Oh, I suppose you think you'd be better off with a man who acts like a doormat? If so, you better think again," Bonnie advised. "Because any man you can control with money or intimidation can just as easily be controlled by someone else. Have you considered what will happen if your grandmother starts rambling and your *Mr. Malleable* is stupid enough to think he can outsmart or outthink her? He won't know what hit him."

Victoria thought of her grandmother, whose diminutive size, soft voice, and impeccable manners often deceived people into thinking she was a pushover. She wasn't. Victoria had named her boutiques *Lavender and Lace* because it reminded her of the strength and durability of her grandmother, who always carried a lace handkerchief and wore a lavender scent. Whomever Victoria introduced as her husband had to be able to hold his own with Clair.

Bonnie crossed her arms in a good imitation of her cousin. "You're right about Kane. He can be controlled about as well as a thunderstorm. But if he likes you, he'll use that same iron will to stand by you no matter what. I'd say he's exactly what you need. Now, are you going to go after him and change his mind or are you going to stand there shaking in your shoes?"

"You know I hate it when you're right."

Bonnie was undisturbed. "Instead of glaring at me, don't you think you better go after Kane?"

Victoria ran for the front door. If anyone had told her an hour ago she would be chasing after a man to get him to marry her, she would have called that person insane. Somehow, once she caught up with Kane, she had to get him to change his mind and help her. If she accomplished that task, she still had a greater challenge of keeping her body from reacting so strongly to his.

He thought she was bothered by his rugged, almost overpowering masculinity. She was, but not in the way he imagined. He was the most riveting man she had ever had the misfortune to meet. He disturbed her in ways she didn't understand and didn't want.

Outside, she saw a mud-splattered truck parked on the other side of the tree-lined street. A man sat inside. His black Stetson-covered head stared straight ahead. One arm was draped across the steering wheel.

Kane. Without hesitation Victoria went to the vehicle and got in on the passenger side.

His head swung around. "What are you doing here, Victoria?"

Neither his eyes nor his voice invited conversation. The tip of her tongue moistened her dry lips. His gaze followed. She felt again the unwanted tightening sensation in the pit of her stomach. "Why . . . why did you stop calling me Tory?"

One large hand clenched and then slowly unclenched on the steering wheel. "I don't think you'd like my answer."

She shifted against the black leather seat. "Kane, I know things didn't work out the way either of us planned, but I had things all worked out in my head and then I met you."

"You're not what I expected either," he drawled, disappointment heavy in his voice.

Victoria decided to ignore his baiting words. "This whole situation is awkward for both of us. Maybe if we got to know each other better."

"I don't think that would help." A flick of his wrist ignited the engine. "If you don't mind, I'd like to be on my way."

She did mind. "I know you want to wring my neck, but—"

"Is that what I want to do to you?" he interrupted, his voice stroking her.

There was no mistaking the husky inflection in

his voice this time. Her heart thudded in her chest. This wasn't supposed to be happening to her.

"Kane, all I want is a business transaction. That way, both parties know where they stand and no one will get . . . the wrong idea."

"We've been through what you want. Now please get out of my truck." *The woman he remembered was gone, and there was no sense staying.*

"I need your help."

"I'm not interested."

"Eleven thousand dollars."

A finger and thumb kicked back his hat. "Not everyone has a price tag. Or is your ego so big you can't stand the idea of a man rejecting you?"

She leaned toward him. "That's the stupidest thing I have ever heard."

"Then get out of my truck."

"No."

"You've got three seconds," Kane warned.

"Twelve thou—"

"Time's up." Strong hands grasped her forearms, twisting and turning her in one deft motion. His mouth captured hers.

Victoria gasped in shock, inadvertently allowing Kane's tongue inside the warm interior of her mouth. Her body stiffened at the unwanted intimacy. But as the velvet roughness of his tongue touched hers, unexpected desire swept through her. She fought the need to join in the kiss until his teeth nipped her lower lip, then suckled the sweet pain away. By the time his mouth covered hers again, she had ceased to think.

Her tongue sought and found his. He tasted hot and sensuous. She had never known a kiss could be so potent. There was nothing she could do to control the fire racing through her body except hold on and try not to be consumed by it. But as their kiss deepened, her own hunger grew, and she made her own demands.

Slim arms circled his neck, knocking his hat off as her fingers plowed through his thick, black hair. From somewhere she heard a moan, then realized it was hers just as a callused palm covered the hard peak of her breast.

Suddenly, her mouth was free.

Her eyes blinked, focused. She lay across Kane's lap, her arms circling his neck. Kane stared down at her, looking as dazed as she felt. The sound of their labored breathing filled the truck's cab.

His hands tightened and his head dipped. Her lips parted.

Kane thrust her away. "God, woman! Don't you have any sense?"

Victoria's trembling hand touched her tingling

lips. *No, she thought, because a man has finally kissed me senseless.*

Briefly, her eyes closed against the unwanted but undeniable truth. Kane had touched her in a way that no man ever had. She didn't like her response, but there was nothing she could do about it.

At least she knew that Kane wouldn't take advantage of her body even if her mind didn't have the sense to say no. She couldn't say the same thing about Stephen or any other man she knew.

She sat up. "I . . . I guess that shows you I'm not scared of you."

"It just shows that neither one of us is thinking clearly," Kane said, the ache in his lower body making him grind his teeth.

Victoria Chandler made a man forget everything except her honeyed skin, sweet lips and tempting body. A man would be a fool to willingly spend time with a woman who could tie his guts in knots. He had lived with that undeniable knowledge for nearly twelve years.

That night, so long ago, during a thunderstorm, he had tried to downplay his reaction to her. He was a man and she was a beautiful young woman. Why wouldn't he feel a healthy dose of sexual attraction? There had been only one problem. Early the next morning after the storm had passed, he had carried the sleeping Victoria to Bonnie's bed and hadn't wanted to let her go.

Disturbed by his desire for a woman he had been sent to protect, Kane made sure he left while she still slept. He stayed away from his aunt and uncle's house for a week. When he returned, Victoria had a new boyfriend.

Kane had gotten on with his life and wished her happiness in hers. Only it hadn't worked out that way. She had married a man who abused her emotionally. Kane now had a second chance to see what might have happened between them.

No other woman haunted his thoughts the way Victoria had. At the oddest times he'd catch himself trying to recall her softness, the scent of her perfume, the sound of her voice. The other women he had dated hadn't helped. He enjoyed them and promptly forgot them. He might feel lust and protectiveness toward them, but he never felt a need to shake the world and make it right for them.

When Bonnie had explained Victoria's problem, he had jumped to help. He hadn't been able to step five feet away from his cousin's front window since six-thirty that night. The first glimpse of Victoria had jolted him. She looked beautiful and frightened and determined. The night of the storm, she had looked the same way. Once again he wanted to slay dragons for her, but she had shrunk from his touch. Each time she pulled away it had been like someone flaying his back with a bullwhip. Yet, he had stood there. Now he needed closure.

He needed to know that the compassionate, sensitive young woman who had been more concerned about her grandparents and Bonnie's welfare than her own safety no longer existed. In her place was a woman who looked no deeper than the surface for a man's worth. He hadn't wasted his time with anyone so shallow since high school.

"Kane, reconsider." Tentative fingers touched his arm. His muscles bunched. This time she didn't pull back. "I need your help."

Kane looked into her rare-colored yellow-green eyes. Cat eyes, soft and pleading and full of passion and need. Just as her body had been against his earlier. Outwardly, she might pretend to be self-assured, but underneath dwelt the same insecure teenager he had held so long ago. And her kiss touched him as nothing ever had.

"I don't know, Tory." She smiled shyly when he said her name and Kane felt the kick in his stomach again.

"I'm glad you're not angry with me any longer. Why don't you come by my place tomorrow and we can have din—" She tucked her bottom lip between her teeth, then glanced away. "Perhaps we should go *out* to dinner." Finding a pencil and paper on the dashboard, she wrote her address and phone number.

"You're going to pretend that kiss never happened?"

"It won't happen again," she said, careful to keep her gaze averted from his face.

"Want to test your theory?"

His voice stroked her. Victoria breathed in sharply. It was a mistake. The scent of his cologne, spicy clean and compellingly sensual, invaded her nostrils. The imprint of his hand lingered on her waist, on her breast. Helplessly, she turned toward him.

"Do you?" he asked.

She was caught between his voice and his eyes, one minute soothing, the next crackling like leashed lightning. "I-I don't want this."

"Your mind may not know what you want, but your body does," he tossed out. Picking up his hat, he rammed it back on his head.

The truth of his words jolted her. "Now who has an ego problem? I know perfectly well what I want—A man who keeps his hands to himself and who does what he's told." Getting out of the truck, she took particular pleasure in slamming the door.

Victoria stalked back into the house and

slammed the front door as well. "Who the hell does he think he is?"

"Your future husband," Bonnie said, her laughter echoing around the high ceiling of the foyer as she unrepentingly turned from spying through the window.

Victoria's glare only made her best friend laugh harder. "Your cousin is the most antagonistic man I have ever met. If there was the slightest hope of finding someone else, I'd tell him to go . . . go jump off a mountain."

"You're just upset because Kane is the only man who hasn't backed down from you."

"Whose side are you on, anyway?"

Bonnie held up her hands as she walked back into the den. "From now on, I'm staying impartial. This is one time I think Cupid could end up getting an arrow in the back."

Chapter 3

Clothes, from beaded and sequined evening dresses to functional day wear in silk and linen and cotton, in various lengths and colors, littered Victoria's king-sized bed. Standing before her mirror, she eyed her red jacket with its matching slim skirt and white shawl blouse, then nodded her head in approval.

The well-cut suit clearly stated the evening was to be a business meeting, not a social one. No more senseless kissing. The word "senseless" caused her to gnash her teeth.

She had been emotionally upset the previous evening. Kane had caught her off guard. This time, however, she planned on keeping the upper hand. Swallowing her pride and asking for his phone number from Bonnie had been bad enough. Then she had had to call twice before Kane had time to talk with her. All he said then was "I'll be there" and hung up.

"If I didn't need you, Kane Taggart, I'd boil you in oil," she said as she applied her lipstick.

Hearing the doorbell, she picked up her red handbag, draped the gold chain strap over her shoulder, and headed for the door. There was no reason to sit and chat. The sooner they left, the sooner she'd know Kane's price. She had found that most men had one.

Taking a deep breath, she opened the door. Her mouth dropped open. Kane, arms folded, leaned casually against the doorjamb as if he had expected her to keep him waiting. He wore a smile on his face as easily as he wore a western-cut gray suit. His gray-and-wine colored tie was silk.

His black eyes captured the reflection of the hall lights and twinkled. "Are you always going to do that when we meet?"

Heat flooding her cheeks, Victoria snapped her mouth shut. A man with eyes that compelling should have to wear dark sunglasses. "You look different."

"You don't," he said, his gaze leisurely running from her black hair in a loose coronet atop her head to her red pumps. "Ready?"

"Yes." Resisting the urge to slam the door again,

Victoria stepped into the hallway. She wasn't vain, but he could have said something about the way she looked after all the time she spent selecting the right outfit. No sooner had the thought materialized than she quickly chastised herself. She didn't care one way or the other what Kane thought about her.

Kane leaned over to test the lock, and for a charged moment Victoria was trapped between him and the door. Her heart rate surged. He smelled of spice and man and danger.

Righting himself, he placed a hand beneath her elbow and started toward the elevator. "Are you always ready for your dates?"

"This isn't a date. It's a business meeting."

"Is that the reason for the suit?" He punched the elevator button, then gave her another leisurely inspection. "That red outfit is sending out mixed messages, or is that what you intended?"

"Mr. Taggart—"

"I thought we dispensed with the formalities yesterday."

"What we shared yesterday was a way of releasing tension. Nothing more," Victoria said tightly.

His index finger slid up and down the shoulder strap of her purse. "I didn't mean the kiss. I meant the reason for our meeting."

"Oh."

Kane smiled and Victoria thought again of boiling oil.

The elevator doors slid open. Bristling, she stepped inside. The man infuriated her. Mixed messages indeed. She didn't want anything beyond a signature from him. Strumming her finger and thumb up and down her purse strap, it took her a few moments to realize she was stroking the exact place he had touched. She jerked her hand away.

Kane leaned against the paneled elevator wall and tried hard to keep the grin off his face. Never in a million years would he have thought he could make Victoria's body sing for him. Sure, he had dreamed; hell, he had even fantasized, but he never really thought it was possible until he had become angry enough to kiss her. He still couldn't believe she had turned to fire and need in his arms.

The night of the storm he had sat in a hallway with Bonnie on one side and Victoria on the other as torrential rain, golfball-size hail, and sixty-mile-an-hour winds beat against his uncle's house. Each time thunder shook the house, Tory burrowed closer to him. Yet despite her own fear, she kept trying to reassure Bonnie. She'd touched him with her compassion.

Bonnie had gone to sleep, but Victoria stayed awake most of the night and they had talked. He learned she was unpretentious and oddly unsure of herself. The lack of confidence in someone so beautiful and wealthy was surprising. He found himself trying to reassure her and holding her just a little bit closer. He had never felt so strong or so helpless as he did that night.

Out of the corner of his eyes, he saw two young women on the elevator whispering and pointing at him. Experience had taught him they were either discussing the best way to come on to him or marveling over his size. He had been born big and grew to a formidable height. Trying out for sports in junior high proved disastrous. He kept tripping over his size-thirteen feet.

It had taken him and his body a long time to come to an understanding. By the time he reached the tenth grade he accepted he wasn't going to wake up one morning and be a cover model unless it was for cigarettes. For whatever reason, all the classically good looks had gone to his younger brother, Matt.

Matt was the pretty boy. Yet they were as close as two brothers could be. That was one reason Kane hated to see Matt so cynical about women in particular and life in general, hated to hear people call him Hard Case.

His brother had two categories for women, the ones you slept with and the ones you called friend. So far, no woman had been able to be both. That didn't stop them from trying. Victoria probably would have gone weak-kneed over Matt, like every other woman. But Kane wasn't giving her the chance to meet Matt until after the wedding.

Kane looked at Victoria again. She was glaring at the two women. He grinned. Imagine, Victoria being protective of him. Apparently she hadn't seen the wink the younger woman had sent him. No matter how Victoria acted, she was a caring woman. And she was going to be *his* woman. If she agreed to his one condition.

"What brought you to Fort Worth, Kane?" Victoria asked mildly.

A black brow arched, then he said, "My horse."

"You rode a horse here?"

He laughed at the incredulous expression on her beautiful light brown face. "I drove a truck. Devil Dancer came in the trailer. He's entered in the calf-roping competition at the National Black Rodeo at the Forth Worth Coliseum."

Astonishment touched her face. "You're a rodeo performer?"

His smile vanished. "You have something against rodeo performers?"

"N-no, of course not. I just assumed . . ."

Kane straightened, giving her his full attention. "Assumed what?"

Victoria glanced around the elevator before she

answered. "I just assumed the cowboy regalia wasn't real."

"Does it bother you knowing it is?"

She beamed. "Oh, no. I'm quite pleased, in fact. Don't some rodeo people follow the circuit year round?"

"Yes, they do," Kane clipped out and watched as Victoria's smile broadened.

The elevator door opened, and people shifted to make room for an oncoming passenger. Something poked Victoria in the side. Frowning, she turned around and looked straight into Mildred Booth's face. Seventy, the old woman swore she was fifty, and was the worst gossip in town. Three years earlier, when the older woman had moved into the apartments, Victoria had seriously considered moving out. Now she wished she had. Unconsciously, she glanced at Kane.

Leaning over, Mildred whispered, "Big and mean looking isn't he? I don't blame you for staring."

Afraid that he might have heard Mildred, Victoria's mouth tightened. "That remark was uncalled for, and I wasn't staring."

Mildred waved Victoria's words aside with a wrinkled hand weighted down with rings on every finger. "High-strung, just like your grandmother. I do hope you're both coming to my party this weekend at the country club." Her voice dropped to a hushed whisper. "Everyone on the 'A' list will be there, including Harold."

"I have plans," Victoria said, staring straight ahead. Harold was Mildred's spoiled nephew, who thought he could buy anything, including a woman.

"My dear, surely you must be jesting," Mildred said, genuine astonishment on her sagging face, layered with powder and rouge. "Harold is one of the most sought-after men in the state."

"Then he shouldn't miss my not being there."

The elevator door glided open on the lobby floor. Passing by Victoria, Kane leaned over and whispered in her ear, "I'll meet you outside." Then he merged with the other passengers.

"Victoria, are you listening to me?"

Irritation flashed through Victoria; to think that she had to ignore Kane because of a gossipy woman like Mildred! "Sorry, I can't come to the party. I do my laundry on Saturdays." She brushed past the openmouthed matron. Victoria's steps quickened as she saw Kane go outside through the revolving glass doors.

Standing on the sidewalk, she quickly scanned the cars lined up in the circular driveway of her high-rise apartment. No truck and no Kane. Feeling foolish and a little put out, she started toward the park across the street. Occasionally, she parked there if all the spaces in front of the building were taken and she didn't have time to park underground.

One of the reasons she moved to the apartment was beautiful Turtle Park. People from all over came to see the five-foot-tall red and white azaleas in bloom, picnic on the lush green grass, or simply watch the ducks meander in and out of the winding stream. At night the park was almost deserted, although lights lit the walkway and shone down from the towering oak trees.

Two trucks were parallel parked in front of the park. One was dented and mud-splattered. The other one was clean. They were both black. Each had a trailer hitch. She bit her lower lip. Yesterday, she really hadn't paid much attention to Kane's truck. All she remembered was that it had been big and black and muddy. Unfortunately, vehicles of the same body style all looked alike to her.

Straightening her shoulders, she started toward the mud-splattered truck. She wasn't afraid of a little dirt or of Kane Taggart, for that matter.

Crossing the street, her heels clicking on the pavement, she went around to the passenger side of the truck and grabbed the handle. The loud, vibrating sound of an alarm blared from the truck's interior. Snatching her hand away, she staggered back.

"Hey, you! Get away from my truck!"

Victoria spun toward the rough voice. Two burly, unshaven men ran out of the park's darkness and into the revealing light. A frisson of fear shot through her. One of them pulled something out of his front pocket and pointed toward the truck. The grating noise stopped. The men, in dirt-smeared jeans, tattered shirts and steel-toed boots, closed in hemming her in between them and the truck.

"Hey, looks like we got lucky," said the one who had shut off the alarm. Rubbing his protruding stomach, he took a swig of beer from a can in his beefy hand. The two men traded laughs and elbow jabs.

Although both men towered over her, Victoria forced herself to relax. "I made a mistake. I thought this was my date's truck."

They jeered and hooted louder. "I heard you uptown babes like to go slumming. Don't chicken out. Me and Sam deserve something soft and nice after working on the high-rise all day."

She averted her head from grimy, questing fingers. "That may be; however, it won't be me. Now please step aside and let me pass."

The man who had spoken moved closer. Stale

beer and body sweat assaulted her nostrils. "What if we don't wanna?"

"Then I'd say you're making a big mistake."

The coldness of the voice caused Victoria and the two men to whirl in unison toward the sound. Kane stood by the back of the truck. "Come here, Tory. They'll let you pass."

Although his stance was casual, there was something menacing and lethal in Kane's glittering black eyes. The men slowly and carefully backed away as if they were afraid any sudden move might make Kane's implied threat a reality.

Trying to mask her relief, Victoria went to Kane. His eyes never left the two men as he placed a possessive arm around her slim waist. Unable to help herself, she leaned into his comforting warmth.

"Apologize to the lady, then be on your way," Kane ordered with icy anger.

"You can't—" started the one who had done all the talking. Kane took his arm from Victoria's waist.

The man held up his hands and stepped back. "Hey, man. I didn't mean no harm to your woman. Sorry, lady."

"I could almost believe you meant it. If I see you bothering another woman, I won't ask for an apology, because when I'm through with you you won't be able to give one," Kane promised with controlled rage. The man's eyes widened in fear.

Kane inclined his head toward the truck. "Get out of here and remember what I said."

The man scrambled around the front end of the truck and jumped inside. His buddy followed. Tires shrieked as the truck left the curb.

Kane didn't speak until the taillights disappeared around the corner. "Are you all right?"

She nodded. "Thank you."

"Do you mind telling me what you were doing bothering that man's truck?" he asked, leading her back across the street.

"I wasn't bothering his truck. Well, I was, but I thought it was your truck," she told him.

"That banged-up thing looks nothing like my truck," he said, stopping beside a gray Mercedes sedan.

"It did to me." At his disbelieving look she continued, "Automobiles of the same style look alike to me. The only way I can tell my car is by the license plate or the stuff inside. You'd be surprised how many red cars there are. I always have to write down where I park." She wrinkled her nose. "The security guards at the area malls know me by name. A couple of them let me park in restricted areas. They say it's easier that way."

Kane looked at her for a long moment, then

burst out laughing. Victoria punched him on the shoulder. He laughed harder. His laugh was worth the last few anxious minutes, she thought. She liked the deep, rumbling sound of it.

Finally, he straightened, forcing himself to stop chuckling. "Does this car look familiar?"

She glanced at the gray car. "It's the same color as Bonnie's, only it's cleaner inside. Is this her car?"

"Not many rodeo performers could earn enough money to own a car like this," Kane said and opened the door.

She started to remind him that if he agreed to marry her, the money she'd pay him would be a nice down payment on a luxury car, then decided to wait until after dinner. "Why didn't you tell me earlier we were going in Bonnie's car?" she asked, getting inside and fastening her seat belt.

Kane waited until he pulled away from the curb before answering. "From what you said, you could have just as easily mistaken another car for it."

"I wouldn't have made that mistake if you would have waited for me," she said accusingly.

Accelerating, he took the entrance to the expressway. "I thought you might not want your friend to know that we were together."

"Mildred Booth is no friend of mine."

"Does the same go for Harold?"

With a feeling of dread, she asked, "Did you hear what Mildred said?"

"With these ears, there isn't much that I miss," Kane said, his voice flat.

Replaying the conversation in her mind, Victoria felt a strange need to touch Kane and reassure him. Knowing he might get the wrong idea, she tried to explain. "Mildred is tolerated only because her late husband was a noted civil rights activist before his death three years ago. She is an unkind woman who still wants to be the center of attention, and she doesn't care who she hurts in the process."

"You haven't answered my question about Harold."

"Harold is her nephew and almost as bad."

Kane sent her a quick glance as he exited the freeway. "Don't you know any good men?"

"No," came her quick reply. She refused to think that that might be her own fault, as Bonnie had pointed out.

"I guess that means I won't have to worry about some man trying to stop our wedding," he said easily.

Her heart thudded. Ignoring the tug of the seat belt, she turned until she faced Kane. "Then you've decided to say yes."

Kane looked at her with unreadable black eyes.

"I've decided to get to know you," he corrected. "Beyond that, I'm not making any promises except one."

"What's that?"

"I always kiss my date good night and, regardless of what you say, tonight you're my date."

Chapter 4

Victoria recoiled. Her heart rate soared. "There'll be no more sen—*unnecessary* kissing."

"It might have been unnecessary, but we both enjoyed it," Kane said bluntly.

"*Tolerated* might be a better word," Victoria said, sitting against the door and staring at the downtown skyline.

"Are you always this dishonest about your emotions or is it just for me?"

Her head whipped around. "You have no right to say anything like that about me."

Kane cut her a quick glance. "Maybe not, but I told you I believe in honesty, and if you want my help, you better remember that."

"Just because I won't stroke your ego, you call me dishonest."

"If I wasn't driving this car, we'd both be stroking something else," Kane said, pulling into the Wellington Restaurant's crowded parking lot.

Victoria's throat dried. "Why do you keep saying things like that?"

Shutting off the motor, Kane unbuckled his seat belt and twisted toward her. "Because I remember a young woman who refused to give in to her fears, yet twelve years later, this same woman has locked herself behind a wall she dares anyone, especially a man, to try and climb over."

The truth of his statement annoyed Victoria. She had cut herself off, but she had never regretted it until now. Kane might have been her friend under different circumstances. "You make me sound like some princess in a tower."

Kane shook his dark head. "A princess wants to be rescued. You're happy locked away from the world. The only thing I can't figure out is why you have to get married."

She watched him wearily. "I thought Bonnie explained everything to you."

"Only what I told you," he admitted and sent her a raking glance. "With a life like yours, you have about as much use for a man as I have for another head."

She opened her mouth to berate him for his cavalier judgment of her, but nothing came out.

Instead, she studied the tight set of Kane's shoulders, the tighter set of his mouth. Thus far, he had asked nothing from her except honesty and she had given him anything but.

He awakened too many old fears. He was closer than he thought in scaling her wall of defense. "You wouldn't understand."

His eyes narrowed. "I might if you told me. I want to be your friend, Tory."

Seeing no way out of her problem, she drew in a deep breath and told him about her grandmother's ultimatum, including her own fabrication of having four men to choose from. She concluded by saying, "I'm as much to blame for this as my grandmother, but I've worked too hard to lose *Lavender and Lace.*"

"I'm your last hope, huh?"

She gripped her purse. Letting Kane know how desperate she was wasn't a good idea, yet her being with him told its own story. "Let's just say I don't see anyone else trying to scale the tower wall."

"Some men are afraid of a few thorns. Come on, let's eat dinner and, if you're nice, I'll pretend not to hear you moan when I kiss you good night."

She had never been so embarrassed in her entire life. After Kane's outlandish remark, the night had gone downhill. They hadn't been seated five minutes before she knocked over her water glass. Each time she looked at Kane his gaze strayed to her lips and her stomach muscles clenched. His velvet laugh made the knot tighten and her annoyance rise. She had barely made it through dinner. She didn't want to feel anything for the man now patiently holding out her door key for her.

"Tory, don't be so hard on yourself. How could you have known that by trying to snatch the check from our waiter you would hit another waiter in the stomach, causing him to drop all those dishes?" The teasing smile on Kane's dark face was in direct opposition to his soothing words. "Don't worry, I left a big tip and paid for all the spilled food."

Victoria gritted her teeth against recalling the shock and humiliation of hearing the waiter's surprised grunt, the ominous sound of clinking china as the plates slid off the tray. Even worse was the memory of Kane literally snatching her out of the way of raining salad, oysters and soup.

"Tomorrow night we'll go someplace where it won't matter if you break every glass in the place," Kane placated.

First thing tomorrow, she thought menacingly, she was going to check on buying a pot of oil. In the meantime, she'd give him his kiss. But she'd give absolutely nothing of herself. "Just get it over with." Shutting her eyes, she tilted her head back.

Something soft and warm brushed against her forehead. Then nothing.

Opening her eyes, she searched for Kane. He was headed for the elevator. Without thought she ran after him. "You come back her, Kane Taggart. For the past hour and a half you had me worried about you kissing me and then you barely touch me?"

He turned. Black eyes twinkled. "Complaining?"

Her head snapped back. "Certainly not."

"I think you are. Tomorrow night we'll do it longer and slower."

"We will not."

"We will if you want my help."

"You're not touching me again."

His gaze darkened with promise. "Wanna bet?"

Gasping, she stepped back. "You are no gentleman."

"I don't remember that as being one of your requirements." Spinning on his heels, he started down the hallway.

"We don't have to go out again. You can tell me your decision now." She'd had all of the man she could stand.

"I never make any important decisions without sleeping on it first. Be ready at nine P.M." He never slowed his pace.

Fury swept through her. She was fighting for her life and he was being stubborn. "You make me so mad I could scream."

Stepping into the empty elevator, he faced her. "Someday I'm gong to make you scream for an entirely different reason."

Her insides clenched. She closed her eyes against the sensual promise in his eyes from thirty feet away. When she had the courage to open them again, he was gone. She groaned. Things weren't working out at all the way she had planned. She had wanted her future husband to be malleable and easily disposed of. Kane was neither. Worse, he was intent on making her sexually aware of him, and so far he was doing a darned good job.

Returning to her apartment, she saw a door a few feet ahead of her close. A tenant had moved in a few weeks ago and Victoria still had not met the new occupant. Mortification caused her to quicken her steps. This was all Kane's fault. Well, tomorrow night she'd show him she was in charge, then she'd get on with her life without a man cluttering it up. Feeling more herself, Victoria gave serious thought to locating a pot for the boiling oil.

*   *   *

Victoria was restocking sachets in an eighteenth
century armoire when she saw them through the
plate glass window of *Lavender and Lace*. Something was wrong. Her grandmother's usually perfect gray hair looked windblown and two of
the buttons down the front of her chiffon dress
were unfastened. The pearls she always wore were
missing—Henry Benson had given them to Clair
on their wedding day and Victoria couldn't remember a single time seeing her grandmother without them.

Her grandfather, who prided himself on wearing dapper-looking ascots, was without one. The
wind lifted his blue sports jacket, revealing the
absence of his trademark red suspenders. Her always impeccably groomed grandparents looked as
if they had dressed in a great hurry. Something disastrous must have happened for them to appear
in public so disheveled.

They hung onto each other as if they were past
their endurance. Worse, her strait-laced grandfather
wasn't stopping at the door, as he usually did. On
an ordinary day, he was embarrassed just looking
at the lingerie-clad mannequins in the window.

Fear propelled Victoria across the room. "What
is it? What's wrong?"

"My poor darling Victoria," cried her grand-mother as she sniffed into a linen handkerchief with a two-inch border of lace.

"I'll beat the scoundrel like the dog he is," Henry Benson flared, his five-feet-five frame quivering with indignation.

Frowning, Victoria looked from one to the other. "What are you talking about?"

"The second cousin to God of course," Clair said, as if her statement made perfect sense.

"Perhaps we should continue this in my office." Victoria turned to the young sales clerk. "Lacy, I don't want to be disturbed."

Leading her grandparents into her office, she sat them on the couch and drew up a chair in front of them. "Now, start from the beginning."

"It's . . . it's all my fault. I never dreamed something like this would happen." Clair leaned her head against Henry's shoulder.

"Grandmother, what are you talking about?"

"The scoundrel you had the argument with last night at your apartment," Henry explained. "We know all about you having to submit to his baseness. Margaret Tillman heard you arguing with him."

"It's my fault." Clair dabbed her teary eyes, but it was clearly a losing battle. "As soon as I hung up the phone from talking with Margaret, we got dressed and rushed over here. Victoria, you must believe me when I say that I never thought things would turn out this way. I can't stop the loan being called in, but there has to be something we can do so you don't have to . . . have to . . ." She looked at her husband for support.

The hand Henry had around his wife's shoulder tightened. He looked at his granddaughter with blazing anger in his brown eyes. "You will maintain your honor."

The pieces clicked into place for Victoria. Apparently Margaret Tillman was the new tenant who had been listening to Victoria's and Kane's conversation. Margaret must not have heard the word "kiss," only words like "touching" and "it." Victoria looked at the two people she loved most in the world and hugged them both. "We were talking about a kiss."

"Margaret said he towered over you and the floor shook when he walked and his voice boomed like thunder," Clair persisted, apparently thinking the description aptly described a celestial being.

"Kane is big, but even he can't shake a sixteen-story building when he walks. His voice is melodious, not boisterous," Victoria said, not realizing her voice had softened. "I wouldn't go out with the kind of man you just described."

Clair and Henry traded glances. Relief visibly

washed over them. Victoria found herself being hugged once again amid murmurs of apology.

"No apology needed. I'm glad you care." Victoria straightened. "Although, I think I'm going to have a talk with my new neighbor. She sounds like a busybody."

"As a matter of fact, she is," Henry admitted. "I guess she wasn't wearing her hearing aid last night. I can't imagine a woman in her sixties being that vain. Mildred Booth recommended the apartment to her."

Victoria threw up her hands. "I knew I should have moved."

"Your marriage should take care of that nicely." Once more in control, Clair placed her handkerchief into her black patent handbag, then set about restoring some semblance of order to her clothes and her hair. Henry did the same.

"Grandmother—"

Clair smiled. "You don't know how you relieved our minds. For a while I thought I might have made a mistake. Might we assume since you're discussing a goodnight kiss that you have narrowed the field without our help?"

Only someone of her grandmother's generation would consider a kiss significant. "You might."

"Is he the cattleman?"

Victoria twisted in her seat. "Yes, Grandfather. He is."

Henry helped Clair to her feet. "Come, Mother, we mustn't overstay. First, I think you forgot something." He pulled a strand of lustrous pearls out of his coat pocket and fastened them around his wife's neck.

Clair took a snowy white neck scarf from her purse and tied it around Henry's neck. For a long moment they shared a special smile.

He turned to Victoria. "We're sorry we doubted you. It will be our pleasure to tell Margaret to mind her own business the next time you and your young man are having a discussion."

Considering she and Kane had a tendency to strike sparks off each other, Victoria thought that might be a wise thing to do.

Gravel crunched beneath the tires of the Mercedes as Kane pulled into a vacant parking space between two trucks. "We're here."

"Here" was the Cuttin' Inn, a country-western dance club. Somehow Victoria wasn't surprised. She glanced around the crowded parking lot. "It's a good thing I didn't try to find your truck here."

"That's a fact," Kane said, loosening his tie.

"What . . . what are you doing?" she asked unsteadily, glancing around the dimly lit parking lot.

"I'm taking enough of a chance going in there wearing dress pants. A coat and tie would send the boys into a fit of laughter so hard they'd probably fall down." He looped the tie over the mirror. "Only thing is that when they got up, they'd tease me into next year."

"These boys are your rodeo friends?"

His fingers hesitated over the top button of his white shirt. "Some of them are. Now, what are we going to do about you?"

"Me?"

"Suits and dance halls don't mix, and if someone got out of hand, I might hit and think later. The double-breasted jacket goes and the hair comes down."

"No. They'll accept me as I am or not at all."

Kane leaned back in his seat. "They'll accept you. I just want them to like the woman I might marry."

Victoria played with the clasp of her handbag. "I was planning on telling as few people as possible."

"Well, that's out. If there is a marriage, my family and friends will be there. Understand that now. That's one thing that's not negotiable," Kane said through stiff lips, his mustache a slash of black.

"You can't have everything your way."

"If I had things my way, you'd be too busy kissing me to do any arguing."

Victoria went hot, then cold. "This is a business—"

"Arrangement. Yeah, I know. So this business partner says we're going inside and dance. Tonight, when you met me at the door with a smile, I thought we might be able to get through one evening without arguing. I guess I was wrong." Opening the car door, he got out and slammed it shut. Victoria winced. Her door opened. "Come on," he said.

Slowly she got out of the car. Kane was right. She had started the evening determined to stop reacting to him emotionally and physically and show him her best side. That was easier said than done. "You, you didn't take off your coat," she stammered.

"It doesn't matter."

Victoria knew why his jacket didn't matter. One look at Kane's face and only someone with a death wish would laugh at him. Besides, he was right about the marriage. If there was one, her grandmother would shout it from the rooftop.

"Don't I have any say in whether we go inside or not?"

"Over my shoulder or walking?"

Kane didn't mince words. Whether she liked it or not, his meaning was out there for you to examine. Where else was she going to find an honest man on such short notice? She needed Kane. She mustn't forget that.

One hairpin, then another came out of her hair until all six were in her hand. Her hair fell into a luxurious black disarray around her shoulders. Putting the hairpins into her purse, she combed her fingers through the dark tumbling mass of curls, then removed her raspberry colored jacket and tossed it onto the front seat.

"Do you always pout when you don't get your way?"

"Men don't pout." His blue coat landed on top of hers. His fingers laced her own. "You'll enjoy the place."

"That remains to be seen. Let's see what the boys have to say about us."

Not a word.

Seven mouths were open, but nothing came out. Their owners were too busy looking. The five men and two women sitting in a curved booth at the back of the huge room hadn't said one word since Kane introduced Victoria as his friend. The only thing that moved were their heads as they looked from Kane to Victoria then back again.

"Are they always like this?" Victoria asked, her

voice raised to be heard over the live band and the male singer's mournful voice lamenting his lost love.

Kane smiled tightly. "I think your beauty has made them speechless. But enough is enough," he said to his friends. "Or you'll make Tory nervous."

The man sitting closest to her jerked his straw hat off his balding pate and scrambled to his feet. The rest, including the two women, followed. "Beg your pardon, Miss Chandler, it's just that Kane never brought a lady—ouch!" He turned to the person who had elbowed him. The man nodded toward Kane.

Victoria's gaze followed. Kane's face was stern and forbidding, his body rigid.

"Pay no attention to Kane," Victoria said. "He's probably unhappy because he wants to dance."

The eyes went back to Kane, their mouths opened. "Is there anything wrong with that?" Kane asked.

Seven heads whipped back and forth.

"No."

"Not a thing."

Victoria took Kane's large hand in hers. "Come on and let's dance, before you turn into a bigger grouch."

Once on the wooden floor, couples swaying around her, her bravado faded. No matter how she tried to pretend otherwise, Kane did strange things to her equilibrium. She didn't understand it, she certainly didn't like it, but it was there nonetheless. "If you'd rather not dance, I'll understand," she said.

"Not a chance." Both hands settled gently on her waist. Victoria tensed in spite of herself. Kane's expression didn't alter. "Look around you, Tory."

She did. Every woman on the dance floor was being held the same way. She looked back at Kane. He waited with the patience of a mountain, apparently undisturbed that people were looking at them oddly because they were just standing there. It was her call. If she stepped into his arms it would imply more trust in him than she had given any man since her divorce. No matter what, she knew she could trust him. She lifted both hands and laced them around his neck. With incredible slowness, he drew her to him.

Awareness ripped through her. The heat of his body seemed to envelope her. Strangely, this time it comforted her rather than made her nervous. She didn't try to analyze why. She simply knew she was tired of being on guard around Kane, and he had proven he'd protect her, even from her own foolish emotions if necessary.

She relaxed and her eyelids drifted shut as his arms tightened around her waist. He moved with surprising ease, his steps sure and graceful. Her cheek rested on his chest. A smile curved her lips at the fast tempo of his heartbeat. Her smile faltered as she realized that he probably felt her erratic heartbeat as well. The music ended and she quickly stepped back and glanced up at Kane.

"Don't look so scared. You're safe . . . for now," Kane said, then winked. A devilish smile on his face, he led her back to the booth.

Several new faces waited for them. Someone pulled up a cane-back chair for her. She sat down and Kane stepped behind her, his fingers curled around the top slat of the chair back, his possessiveness obvious.

This time, no one had any difficulty talking. With a firm handshake and a smile, people introduced themselves. The names of their hometowns were as varied as the hues of their skin.

Surprise widened Victoria's eyes on learning that the short barrel of a man who had the courage to speak first was a "bullfighter." Ben said he preferred that name over "rodeo clown." Victoria agreed once Kane explained Ben's job was to protect bull riders by playing dodge with two-thousand-pound angry animals.

Not to be outdone, the men who were bareback riders, steer wrestlers, and calf ropers were just as vocal. Jason, Oklahoma Slim, and Manuel got into an argument over who had won more belt buckles in previous competitions. Victoria glanced at Kane's waist and he shook his head.

"This time I bet you'll win one," she whispered, then turned her attention to Stony, a muscular young man with a wad of chewing tobacco stored in his cheek.

"I'm going to be the best pickup man in the business." Stony shifted the tobacco to the other cheek, then continued, "When the eight-second buzzer goes off and a man's lucky or skilled enough to still be ridin' a buckin' bronc and he's lookin' for a way off, I'll be there to lift him off as gently as if he were a baby."

Victoria saw the determination in the man's eyes and wished him luck. She soon learned some of the people were in town for the rodeo, others lived nearby. Everyone seemed to respect and defer to Kane. Victoria sensed it had nothing to do with his size. He was genuinely well liked and respected. Somehow she wasn't surprised.

Someone pushed a beer into her hand. Not wanting to remark that she didn't like beer, she accepted the foaming mug with a smile. After several minutes had passed and she hadn't taken a drink, Kane took the glass. She glanced over her shoulder and smiled her thanks, then turned to see everyone staring at her again.

"I'm afraid it didn't work, Kane."

His large hand tensed on her shoulder. "What didn't work?"

"Leaving our jackets in the car. We're still somewhat of an oddity, the way we're dressed," she said with wry amusement.

"No," a pretty brunette rushed to say. "I've been admiring your outfit." She looked at Kane. "Since I know you won't punch a woman, I might as well tell Victoria, before she thinks we all have fallen off our horses one time too many."

"Penny, some things are more dangerous than barrel racing," Kane answered.

Uncertainty crossed the young woman's face. Victoria hadn't seen Penny, an insurance adjuster from Oklahoma, so quiet since they were introduced. The other woman by her side appeared just as unsure of herself. Victoria stood. "Penny, could you and Kisha show me to the ladies room?"

Smiling sweetly into Kane's scowling face, Victoria linked arms with the two women. Five minutes later she had discovered that Kane hadn't brought another woman to the Cuttin' Inn in over two years, and when he had, they hadn't danced. The knowledge saddened her. Hadn't any other woman had the sense to recognize what a good man Kane was?

Penny must have read the expression on Victoria's face, because she said, "Don't think it's because he hasn't had the opportunity. He has. He's just particular. Kane's not the type of man to date just to have a woman on his arm. Unlike his brother, Matt, who changes women faster than he can rope a calf. He was the '91 champion."

Victoria frowned. "Kane didn't mention he had a brother."

"Kane nor any other man with good sense," Kisha said, repairing her lipstick. "Matt's as handsome as sin and he has a smile that could make an angel weep." She sighed. "His black eyes will make your heart go into overtime, *if* you're lucky enough to catch his eye."

"Catching his eye is not the problem. Keeping it on you is," Penny said. She and Kisha shared a look.

It was evident that both of the women had tried to interest Matt. Obviously they hadn't been successful.

Penny glanced at Victoria. "You're lucky to have a stable man like Kane."

"You make him sound as dull as week-old dishwater," Victoria said, aware that she sounded defensive.

The two women laughed. Kisha shook her head.

"Kane? Dull? Cross him or do something to one of his friends and see how dull he is. Most men would rather tangle blindfolded with a bear than get on Kane's bad side. Like Penny said, you're lucky."

Victoria followed them out of the ladies' room, her mind on Kane. What had possessed her to take up for him? He could take care of himself. As for her being lucky . . . her luck had run out six months ago.

"You all right?"

Victoria looked up to see Kane standing near the end of the fifty-foot bar. She saw something she never expected to see in his eyes . . . uncertainty. It touched her as nothing had in years. "You have some very loyal friends. You're a fortunate man."

The tension seemed to ease out of his broad shoulders. He took her hand. "Come on. Since you said you never learned the "Cotton-Eyed Joe," the boys decided to have the band do it in your honor."

She grinned and held up her full skirt. "Lead on."

When the line went forward, Victoria went backward. Dancers kicked forward, she kicked backward. Kane never stopped laughing. His warm laughter flowed over her, through her, making it harder to concentrate. Finally, his powerful arm circled her waist and held her against the hard line of his body with an easy strength that fascinated and amazed her.

"Put your arm around my neck, honey," he grinned.

She did, despite the tingling in her body, despite the people in the line behind her and on her line shouting that she and Kane were cheating. Once or twice she asked Kane to put her down. He did, until she made a misstep and back up she went. When the dance ended, she still had one arm looped around his neck.

People circled around them, applauding. She hadn't had so much fun in years. With a start, she realized she had also forgotten the reason she was out with Kane. On some deeper level, she didn't fear or distrust Kane as she did other men. She didn't know whether to be pleased or not.

Reluctantly, Kane put her on her feet. One possessive arm remained around her waist. "I'm going to get Tory something to drink. She's probably thirsty from all that dancing," Kane said, a wide grin on his dark, craggy face.

Catcalls and good-natured jeers followed them to the bar. Victoria slid onto a wooden stool. Kane hooked one booted heel over the chrome footrest circling the bar and stood beside her.

"What will you and the lady have, Kane?" the bartender asked, wiping the scarred oak surface of the bar with a dry cloth.

"A diet cola," Victoria replied.

"A diet cola and a long neck, Jake."

Nodding, the bearded man turned away. Kane gently brushed the wisps of black hair off her forehead. "You really are having a good time."

Before she could answer, a tall glass clinking with ice cubes and a bottle of beer were plunked on top of cardboard coasters. She took a sip of cola. "You doubted?"

He rolled the bottle between finger and thumb. "I wasn't sure. I just wanted to bring you here."

"Why?"

"These are my friends. I wanted to see if you could be comfortable with them and them with you."

She tilted her head to one side and stared up at him. "I might have believed that two hours ago, but not now. You respect and like your friends, but you wouldn't care two hoots and a holler, as Penny would put it, what they thought about the woman in your life."

"You think so?" He took a swig of beer.

"I know so. Now, care to tell me the real reason we're here?"

For a long moment he stared at the foam disappearing in the brown bottle, then his gaze captured hers. "I wanted to hold you, and the only way I could think of was to take you dancing."

She felt humbled, special, and in trouble. She searched her mind for something to say and could think of nothing that wouldn't lead him on or hurt him. Her grateful gaze touched the beer bottle. "Thanks for taking my beer earlier. I can't stand the taste."

Kane spluttered, almost choking as he jerked the long-neck bottle out of his mouth. Alarmed, Victoria jumped off the stool to pat him on the back. "Are you all right?"

"Yeah." The bottle thumped on the bar. "Must have gone down the wrong way." Pulling out some bills, he laid them beside the discarded beer. "Ready to go back to your place?"

"Yes," she said, realizing instantly why Kane had stopped drinking his beer. The good-night kiss. Did he plan to kiss her on the mouth tonight? She had certainly acted like they were on a date. Her body tensed. Whether it was in fear or anticipation, she didn't know, and she wasn't going to look too deeply for the answer.

They walked back to their table and said their goodbyes. To requests that she come to the rodeo starting in two days, she gave a noncommittal "I'll see."

Becoming better acquainted with Kane's friends wasn't a a good idea. If Kane agreed to help her, the least she could do was save him the awkward embarrassment of trying to explain what had happened to her after the divorce . . . as she had had to explain about Stephen.

Neither spoke on the way to her apartment. The only sound was the country and western music on the radio. Every song described a broken-hearted woman or man that was cheated on or left behind.

"Aren't any country and western songs happy?" Victoria asked, the lyrics increasing her nervousness.

"Some are, but I guess most of the time you have to hurt before you know what it is to love."

She glanced at him as he pulled under the covered driveway. "Have you ever been hurt?"

"Once."

"What happened?"

"She married someone else," he said softly.

The sadness in his voice tore at her heart. "I'm sorry."

"No sorrier than I am." He switched off the engine. "Come on. I guess it's time we talked."

Kane opened his door, feeling the tension back in his body again. In a matter of minutes he'd either lose or win the only woman he wanted for his wife. Victoria had her jacket back on, but her hair was still down. His hands itched to run his fingers through that hair, shimmering in the light, but he knew he couldn't. Not yet.

His hand gently rode the curve of her waist as they entered the elevator. Feeling her stiffen, he withdrew his hand and stepped back. Maybe he was crazy thinking his plan could work. But what did he have to lose? On the sixteenth floor, the doors slid open and they stepped off.

Inside the living room, Victoria asked, "Can I get you anything?"

"No." Kane looked around the room. Chic and stylish and feminine. It reflected the woman, with soft colors of peach and ivory and blue. There was nothing soft about him or the life he led, yet he wanted her to share that life.

Victoria sat on the sofa and took a deep breath. "What is your decision?"

Kane rammed his hands in his pockets, then just as quickly ripped them out again. "The decision will be yours, once I tell you what I want."

Something inside her heart twisted. "You mean you want more money. Is fifteen thousand dollars enough?"

"It isn't money I want."

She swallowed. "Then what is it, Kane? What do you want?"

"You, Tory. I want you to be my wife for real."

Chapter 5

Shock ripped through Victoria, widening her eyes, sending her heartbeat soaring. He reached for her. She shrank back in the chair.

"No. I-I told you I wanted a busi—"

"Forget the business agreement," Kane said fiercely. "I'm asking you to be my wife."

Panic-stricken, she rose. Her legs trembled. Blindly, she groped for the back of the couch to steady herself. "Kane, I don't want this."

"You think I don't know that? It's all I've thought about all night. Do you think I'd choose for a wife someone who can't decide if she wants to run *to* me or *away* from me?"

Victoria was too stunned by his counteroffer to try and explain the reasons behind her erratic behavior. "I'll double the money."

"I don't want your money. I want a wife."

She shook her head in bewilderment.

Kane clenched his fists to keep from dragging her into his arms. "Listen, Tory. I'm not some crazed fool who is going to abuse you or take advantage of you. You're Bonnie's friend, for goodness's sake. The first time I saw you at your and Bonnie's commencement, the other girls wore dresses, you wore a collarless white suit with a single strand of pearls and pearl earrings. Your hair was up. The whole family had come up for Bonnie's graduation."

"I don't remember seeing you."

"Would it have made any difference if you had?"

Victoria wanted to tell him that she would have smiled, but she knew at eighteen, she had been eager to test her womanhood. Kane had held her and soothed her fears, and she had never thought to seek him out and say thank you. At the time, she had been too busy with a new boyfriend. Stephen had taught her that cruelty worked both ways.

"You trusted me the night of the storm twelve years ago," Kane said softly. "Trust me again. Marry me, Tory. I'll make you a good husband."

She shook her head, her hand clutching her churning stomach. "I told you what I expected from you. I don't need a good husband. I only need a signature."

"What about someone to care for you, laugh with, share your dreams with?"

His voice, soft and coaxing, reached out to her. Her spine stiffened. "I don't need caring. I have my boutiques."

"Then what about what you feel when I hold you?" he asked gently. If he could get her to stop running from her feelings long enough to face them, they might have a chance.

Her churning stomach worsened. "I admit there's an unexplained 'something' between us, but I don't plan to give in to it or act on it."

He studied her for a long moment, his fist tightening. He had lost. He didn't want a woman whose barriers he had to knock down every moment they were together. Without trust, they had nothing to build on. "I don't guess you could have made it any plainer."

"Kane, I need you."

"What about *my* needs, Tory? Have you for one moment considered my feelings?"

"I offered you money," she wailed. Didn't he understand? Money was the only thing she could give him that wouldn't put her emotionally at risk.

Black eyes blazed. "I'm not Stephen. I want to give, not take."

The throbbing sincerity in his voice made her throat sting. "Don't you understand? I can't give in return. I don't know how and, even if I did, I won't be that vulnerable again."

Kane's face softened. "You're wrong, Tory. You give just by being you. I saw the way you looked at those two women on the elevator, the way you made my friends feel at ease around you. You have so much to give if you'd just let yourself."

"I'm not so giving that I'm going to jump into bed with you to save my business!"

"Your body is as hungry as mine, Tory. We both know it!" Kane's voice curled through her.

"Will you stop saying things like that? A few kisses doesn't prove anything."

Kane took a step closer, his eyes dark and compellingly sensual. "How many men have you kissed like you kissed me?"

Victoria ran a distracted hand through her hair and looked away from the temptation of Kane's mouth. "That's not the point. Anyway, what would you do with a wife while you're following the circuit?"

"I'm not with the rodeo," he said softly.

"What?" As if her legs were unable to hold her any longer, she sank into a chair. Her head bowed, her trembling fingers massaged her pounding temples. Kane kept throwing her one curve after the other.

Black cowboy boots came into her line of vision. Her head jerked up. "What is it you do?"

"I have a small place about a forty-five-minute drive from Fort Worth."

She looked at him with accusing eyes. "You could have told me that instead of letting me think you were a rodeo performer."

"You seemed to like the idea of my not being around. Besides, it doesn't matter what I do unless we can come to a compromise."

She sat up straighter. "What kind of compromise?"

"I still want a wife." He held up his hand when she opened her mouth to speak. "However, I'm willing to admit that asking you to be my wife for real might have been taking advantage of your situation. But, remembering how you kissed me, I didn't think you'd fight so hard." Victoria's back became straighter. "Therefore, I'm willing to give you your own bedroom. In return, you'll live with me for the length of our marriage. To the outside world, you'll be my wife."

"Live with you! I can't do that. I have a business to run."

"If you don't get married in sixteen days, there won't be a business," Kane reminded her.

For a moment, Victoria was speechless. How

dare he use her deadline on her! The pounding in her temples began anew.

"Look at it from my viewpoint, Tory. People are going to talk anyway when they learn we married so quickly. If you stay in Fort Worth while I stay in Hallsville, people will have a field day. With all that talk, your grandmother is bound to become suspicious."

"What do you get out of it?"

He smiled wistfully. "A wife. Someone to worry about me if I'm late, have coffee with in the morning, share the day with."

"I'd be a substitute for the woman you lost?" she asked.

Once again his face became shadowed. "What does it matter as long as you get my signature on a marriage license?" When no answer came, his face strengthened into resolve. "I'll stick around until noon tomorrow. After that I'm gone and I won't be back."

She stood. Her hand clenched the back of her chair. "Twenty thousand dollars."

He countered. "Six months in my house in your own bedroom."

Again she ran a distracted hand through her hair. "Why can't you be sensible and understand that what you're asking for is impossible?"

"I understand more than you think I do. You're

still locked behind the tower and letting Stephen run your life."

"That's crazy. I hadn't spoken to him in over two years until he called last week. His life is going down the drain and he obviously thought I was foolish enough to care. He was wrong. I can barely stand to be in the same room with him."

Kane's eyes darkened. "Or any other man. You've let your hatred for him dictate your reactions to everything. Instead of being thankful you wasted only eleven months of your life, you keep it before you like a mirror."

Her temper flared. "You can't stand there and judge me. You don't know what it was like. He made my life hell, then left me with nothing."

"Tory, stop feeling sorry for yourself. Your marriage to Stephen made you stronger, not weaker." His gaze bore into her. "Do you think you would have had the courage to go against your grandparents' wishes and start your stores if living with him hadn't made you stronger?"

"How do you know—" she started to ask him, then knew the answer. "How much has Bonnie told you about me?"

"It was less than I wanted. She's your friend first, my cousin second. Cheer up, Tory. Maybe the next man will free you for good." The door closed softly behind him.

Hands clenched by her side, Victoria headed to her bedroom. The phone rang as she passed the end table.

"Yes," she snapped, then grimaced at her caustic tone.

There was a long pause before the caller said, "I guess I don't have to ask if tonight went any better than last night."

Victoria plopped in a chair. "No, Bonnie, you don't. Kane wants me to live with him. In separate bedrooms."

"Seems reasonable to me. After all, you're asking him to give up other women. The least you can do is keep him company," Bonnie pointed out.

"I might have known whose side you'd be on."

Bonnie laughed softly. "I told you, I'm staying out of this. I love you both."

"Bonnie, why didn't you ever mention Kane was asking questions about me?" Victoria fretfully twirled the telephone cord around her finger.

"Didn't seem important, I guess. Kane is easy to talk to, and I admit I worried about you when you and Stephen were married. But you know I'd never betray a confidence," Bonnie hastened to add.

Victoria did know. She had told Bonnie more about herself than anyone else in the world, but there was one shameful secret Victoria would never tell anyone. "Kane docs have a way of slipping past your defenses."

"But he'd never use it against you."

"Tell that to someone he isn't trying to black-mail."

Laughter floated through the receiver again. "Good night. I want a full report tomorrow."

"Good night." Victoria hung up the phone and stared at the front door. He'd be back. No man would give up twenty thousand dollars to live with her for six months.

"Victoria, you're going to rip the lace décolleté if you aren't careful. Why don't you just take off the arm, as you usually do?"

Slender fingers clutched the silk chartreuse camisole briefly, then continued to ease the spaghetti strap up the arm of the mannequin. "Did you need something, Grandmother?" Victoria asked.

Clair's sigh was loud and eloquent. "I thought you might be a little put out with me. My lawyer called this morning."

Victoria picked up the matching floral kimono and began slipping it on over the chemise. "Why should I be a 'little put out' as you call it just be-cause I received a certified letter this morning giving me fifteen days to repay a loan of two hundred and fifty thousand dollars or turn over the keys to my stores?"

"Dear, you know that won't happen, because you're going to be married by then." Clair thoughtfully fingered the pearls at her throat. "You did take into consideration the length of time it's going to take to get the marriage license and blood tests, didn't you?"

Victoria turned, her yellow flared shirt swirling around her legs. Her headache was back with a vengeance. "Grandmother, was there something you needed?"

"No, not really. I called last night and didn't get an answer. I guess you were out with your cattleman again. All those late hours are putting circles under your eyes."

The tenuous hold on her patience snapped. "He's not my cattlema—"

She pivoted as the little gold bell over the stained glass front door jangled. Two young women came in and Victoria's assistant, Lacy, moved to help them. Victoria's hands clenched. Her gaze strayed to the wall clock. 10:45.

"What do you mean he's not your cattleman? Did you have another fight? Is that why you keep looking at the front door every time the bell rings? Is he coming here?" Clair asked in an excited rush.

"No, Grandmother, that's not what it means."

"What is it, dear? I haven't seen you this upset since you discovered Stephen was being unfaithful." Clair gasped. "He isn't married, is he?"

"No."

Clair relaxed. "For a moment you had me worried. Don't think this entire matter hasn't disturbed me." Frail fingers touched Victoria's cheek. "You're all I have left of your dear father, all the hopes and dreams of the Chandlers rest with you. For all of us, you have to remarry."

Feelings of dread climbed up Victoria's spine. There was no way out of the web of lies she had helped spin. "If I don't?"

Fear darkened Clair's eyes and pinched her lips. "Then you will lose *Lavender and Lace* and I will lose you." Tears sparkled in the older woman's brown eyes. "I don't see how I could stand that."

Fighting her own tears, Victoria hugged her grandmother's small frame to hers, smelled her familiar lavender scent, felt her grandmother's arthritic hands try to squeeze her granddaughter into acceptance. If Victoria lost the shops, there would be no winners.

Choices were gone.

Kane's counteroffer flashed through her mind. She shied away from the thought of living with him. Not because the thought repulsed her, but because it didn't. She didn't want anything in her life she couldn't control. But she no longer had the luxury of having things her way.

Gently pulling away, Victoria opened her grandmother's black patent purse, found the lace handkerchief she knew would be there and dried her grandmother's eyes. "Everything will be all right."

Clair looked doubtful. "Are you sure?"

"Yes." Victoria answered with more assurance than she felt. Sealing her fate, she said, "I'm seeing him today."

"When can we meet him? Does he come from a big family?"

Victoria answered the only question she knew the answer to. "I'll see if he can come to the dinner party you're having tonight."

"Please assure him he'll be welcomed." Clair shook her graying head. "I'll need a distraction with your grandfather's side of the family there."

"He may have other plans," Victoria pointed out quickly.

Clair gave Victoria one of her stubborn looks. "Then it's up to you to change them." She tugged on her white lace gloves. "One question?"

"No, you don't know him."

"That wasn't the question."

"All right."

"Has he kissed you senseless yet?"

Victoria's cheeks flushed. Her hands flew up to palm her face, but it was too late. Her grandmother smiled and began humming the wedding march from *A Midsummer Night's Dream*. The boutique's front door closed softly behind her.

One hour, three phone calls, and two wrong turns later, Victoria pulled her red Jaguar into the back parking lot of the Fort Worth Cowtown Coliseum holding the National Black Rodeo. Trucks and trailers, in every description and size, from chrome-plated and air-conditioned to faded and dented, littered the area.

Stepping out of her car, her nostrils were assaulted with the earthy scent of cattle and horses. Recalling the statue of Bill Pickett, the first black rodeo performer, at the entrance to the coliseum, her uneasiness returned. The inventor of bulldogging was portrayed biting the lips of a steer as he brought it down. Apparently rodeo performers were unique individuals, and so were the men who worked with them. Brushing an unsteady hand over her white suit, she started toward the bold red entrance sign to find Kane.

The white leather heels of her pumps clicked on the hot pavement. Dressing in white to remind

Kane of their meeting years ago had been her last-ditch effort to sway him, although Kane didn't strike her as a man easily influenced.

"It's about time you came to rescue us."

Victoria glanced around to see Penny. With her was a man wearing jeans and a blue chambray shirt. The brim of a black Stetson shaded the upper part of his brown-skinned face.

"Hello, Penny," Victoria greeted. "What are you talking about?"

"Kane. He's been as grouchy as a bear." She glanced at the tall man beside her. "Victoria Chandler meet Matt Taggart, Kane's brother."

Victoria's gaze swung back to the silent man. His nut-brown face was unbelievably handsome, yet no warmth shone from his piercing black eyes. He was as still as a shadow and appeared to be as unfeeling. She found nothing but his black eyes and powerful build to indicate any relation to Kane. She couldn't see what fascinated Penny about him.

"Hello, Matt."

"So, you're the one," Matt said, his voice low and deep, his eyes studying hers intently.

"The one what?" Victoria asked. When Matt didn't answer, just continued to study her with unblinking black eyes, she dismissed him and asked Penny, "Can you tell me where I can find Kane?"

"I'll take you to him," Matt said.

His offer surprised Victoria, since he had yet to show any friendliness toward her. "Penny can show me."

"She needs to practice and Kane is in a restricted area. If you want to see him, you'll have to go with me." Without looking at the other woman, Matt asked, "Penny, don't you think you should get going?"

After one longing look at Matt, Penny left. Victoria felt sorry for the other woman because Matt seemed to have already dismissed her from his mind.

"To have attracted Kane's attention, there must be more to you than a beautiful face," he said bluntly.

"From what I've heard about you, I can't say the same," Victoria tossed back.

He laughed, a gravely noise that sounded as if he hadn't laughed in a long time. Victoria's eyes widened at the change it made in his face. It was wickedly sensual. At last she saw the fire behind the shadow. Women would line up in droves to draw the real man from behind his facade. Yet she wouldn't try for all the gold in Fort Knox. That kind of man would leave you crying and never even notice there were tears on your cheeks.

"Come on. Penny's right about Kane. Let's go put him out of his misery."

They followed the white fence until they came to the gate of a small arena. As soon as Matt opened the gate, Victoria saw Kane. Her heart rate kicked into overtime. Arms folded, he leaned back against the fence. He didn't look any happier than she felt.

Matt let out an ear-piercing whistle. "Kane, a lady is here to see you."

Kane glanced up. He and Victoria's gaze met, held. His expression softened. Pushing away from the fence, he took several running steps then stopped abruptly. His face became hard and shuttered as he looked from her to Matt, who was holding her arm.

"I think I'd better leave. So long, Victoria." Tipping his Stetson, Matt walked away.

Uncertainty kept her from moving. Thirty feet separated her from Kane, yet neither moved. Then he started toward her again. Too nervous to smile, she clutched the strands of perfectly matched pearls around her neck.

"What's your answer?"

"You're asking too much."

"Of which one of us? Is it asking too much for a wife to spend six months out of a year with her husband or too much for a husband to give up the pleasure of his wife's bed?" He glanced at his watch. "Make your decision, Tory. It's twelve, straight up."

Chapter 6

"Why do you want a woman interfering in your life, asking you to take out the garbage, pick up your clothes, wash the car?"

"You're evading the issue and you know it," Kane responded smoothly.

Knowing that Kane easily saw through her diversion didn't help. Victoria swallowed. "How about a week?"

"Goodbye, Tory." Gently he pushed her out of the way and closed the gate. He turned away with her looking through the slats.

Just keep walking, Kane told himself. Put one foot in front of the other.

His body obeyed, but that didn't help the pain twisting his gut. He hadn't realized how much he wanted her to say yes until she turned him down.

He had gambled and lost the only woman he had ever loved. Before the kiss in his truck he only wanted a woman who had haunted his thoughts. Somewhere between then and now, desire had strengthened into love. When it happened didn't matter. He loved a woman who was afraid to love.

He knew himself well enough to realize that having Victoria for a wife and not being able to touch her would have slowly killed him inside. But it would have been worth the gamble to get her to love him and share his life.

Maybe it wouldn't hurt so bad if he didn't know she was fighting her attraction to him. No matter what she said, she still judged every man by Stephen. And until she took the first step to put her ex-husband behind her, she'd never be free to love Kane or any other man.

It was time he left Fort Worth and went back to his ranch. Victoria wasn't going to change her mind and he wasn't going to change his. But the plunging neckline of her suit jacket had almost done him in.

From his height he could detect a bit of white lace against the rounded curve of her honey-colored breasts. If that wasn't enough of a temptation to Kane, her skirt reached six inches above her beautiful knees. Lord, but he had almost been enticed into swallowing his pride and taking her on any terms.

The chute across the arena opened, and out burst a three-hundred-pound calf. Matt, riding Devil Dancer, was right behind the animal. With a practiced twist of his wrist, Matt widened the rope's noose as it twirled over his head. At the exact moment he released the twenty-five-foot lariat, the back Angus spun in the opposite direction.

He missed by three feet. Knowing a second loop took precious seconds and usually kept the roper from receiving prize money, Matt didn't attempt another throw. To the sound of good-natured jibes and instructions, Matt took the slack from his rope, the animal forgotten. All the men knew the calf would run for the gate expecting to get out as was the customary practice during a real rodeo event.

All except Victoria.

Please, don't have followed me this time. Even as Kane thought the words, he turned. What he saw made his heart stop. Victoria, standing in the gate, looking at him.

"Get out of the way!" he yelled, and started running, calling out for Matt.

Finally, Victoria saw the black streak running straight toward her. Instead of moving, she screamed one word, "Kane!"

Booted feet pounded the dirt-filled arena. Animals were unpredictable. The calf might veer around Victoria but it could just as likely run over her. Knowing he had one slim chance to keep Victoria from possible injury, Kane kept his eyes on the Angus, praying he'd intercept the animal before it reached Victoria.

His heart hammering, his lungs bursting from want of air, Kane ran. Just a few more feet.

Determined hands grabbed around the animal's neck. The calf immediately protested by bucking and twisting sideways toward the unwanted obstruction. Kane hung on, digging his heels into the dirt-filled arena and twisting the calf's head back, its nose up.

Both elbows ripped through Kane's white shirt sleeves. The animal went down and didn't move.

Matt jumped off his horse while the chestnut was going full speed. Using "piggin string," Matt tied three legs of the downed calf in two seconds.

Kane's midnight eyes blazed as he stood and faced his brother. "What the hell do you mean letting the damn calf get away?"

"He ran for the gate. I didn't know she was there."

"You shouldn't have brought her here!"

"Kane, do you really want to tear a strip off me or see to your woman?" Matt asked calmly.

"She's not my woman!"

"And it's eating you up inside."

Kane raised his fist. The younger man didn't flinch. "I'd let you beat hell out of me, big brother, if I thought it would make you feel better. It won't. Take Victoria to my trailer."

Kane looked at Victoria. What he saw made his gut twist violently again. Her face was pinched in fear. Her arms were folded protectively around his damn hat, her purse lay a few feet away.

He grabbed her purse in one hand and her elbow in the other.

His hands were trembling, but his voice was as sharp and as biting as a bullwhip. "I told you to go home. Don't you ever think before you do something?"

He stalked through the open gate without a backward glance. "Everyone knows how unpredictable animals are, and nobody but a fool would stand in front of the gate unless they know how to scale a fence."

Going up the steps of a trailer home, he opened the door and pushed her inside. "Can you scale a fence, Tory?"

She mutely looked at him.

Without benefit of undoing the buttons, he tore the ruined shirt from his body leaving only his white tee shirt. He twisted the faucet on the kitchen sink and water gushed froth. He washed his hands. Finished, he jerked a paper towel. The entire roll hit the floor.

He cursed.

She whimpered.

His hands fisted.

His angry gaze settled on his hat. "Stop clutching that damned hat," he ordered. Snatching the Stetson from her fingers, he flung it to the floor. "It doesn't mean a thing to me. It can't feel pain . . . it can't . . ."

His eyes closed, his hands shook. He drew in a ragged breath.

"Kane, if you're going to fuss, do you possibly think you could do it while you're holding me?" Her voice was a wobbly thread of sound.

"Oh, God, Tory. If I touch you . . ."

She bit her lip. If Kane didn't put his arms around her, she was going to lose what little control she had managed to hang onto. She needed to feel his strength. "P-please," she whispered. "I—" Her voice broke.

He swept her into his arms, felt her body tremble. His arms tightened. "You're safe, honey. Don't cry." He sat on the couch because he wasn't sure how much longer he could stand. He settled her in his lap. "I'm sorry for yelling. Don't cry, honey. The calf probably would have ran on past you. I'll bet being bulldogged scared him as much as he scared us." Knowing he shouldn't, yet unable to help himself, Kane kissed her eyelids, the curve of her lips.

"I-I don't think that's possible. I was so frightened."

"I should have made sure you were safe." Self-condemnation laced his voice.

She pushed away from his chest and studied his dark brown face. "It wasn't your fault." Trembling fingers tenderly stroked his cheek again and again as if in reassurance. "It was mine. I shouldn't have followed you." Her body shuddered. "If anything had happened to you, I never would have forgiven myself."

Ebony eyes held hers. "You were scared for me?"

"When you grabbed that animal, all I could think of was that if you were hurt it was because you were trying to protect me. You told me you weren't a rodeo performer." She swallowed. "Kane, I know you're probably tired of hearing it, but I am sorry."

"Now that you're safe and my heart is out of my throat, I'm not. I got you into my arms again." His hands stroked the curve of her back. "If you don't want to be thoroughly kissed, speak now or be prepared not to speak for a long time."

Victoria glanced up through tear-spiked lashes. "I don't think we should."

"Probably not, but we are if you aren't off my lap in three seconds and counting."

Knowing how much she wanted to stay gave her the will power to move from the security of his arms onto the couch.

Kane immediately pushed to his feet. "If you're feeling better, I'll help you find your car."

She didn't move. Instead she watched Kane pick up the roll of paper towels and slip them back into the holder. Despite her refusal of his counteroffer, he had not hesitated to protect her from danger, then from himself. He always put her first.

How many men wouldn't have taken advantage of her vulnerability or would have remembered she needed help in locating her car? How many men would be that generous or caring? Kane deserved better from her than she had given him.

The words began softly, cautiously, then gathered strength and momentum. "*Lavender and Lace* is the only thing I've ever been successful at. Mother finished summa cum laude at Spelman; Daddy finished magna cum laude at Morehouse. They were number five and six in their med-school graduating class at the University of Texas.

"My parents balanced their social and professional lives as skillfully as they wielded a scalpel. They lectured all over the country. The best I ever did was the seventieth percentile. They never said anything, but I always felt somehow I had let them down." She closed her eyes for a moment, then focused on her clasped hands in her lap.

"They died in a boating accident when I was twelve. I went to live with my flamboyant grandmother and indulgent step-grandfather who loved me, but again I was overshadowed. I couldn't get over the feeling that I should be smarter, wittier, prettier." She looked up and met Kane's intense gaze without faltering.

"I met Stephen when I was a junior in college. He was handsome, a smooth talker, and a hustler. He made me feel important. I got a marriage license instead of the degree in business I always wanted." Her lashes lowered, concealing the pain in her eyes. "*Lavender and Lace* is the only thing I'm good at."

Kane was stunned by Victoria's confession. He remembered sensing her insecurities the night of the storm, and couldn't believe she hadn't outgrown them. Despite her devastating divorce, despite her grandparents' wishes to the contrary, she had taken charge of her life, stood on her own feet and succeeded.

"My life revolves around my stores. I'd do anything to save them except put myself at risk emotionally. You want something from me I can't give," she finished softly.

Kane heard the fear and vulnerability behind Victoria's words and wanted nothing more than to lift her chin, pull her into his arms, and kiss her until she was breathless and aching with desire. But that was what she was afraid of . . . the mindlessness that overtakes a woman when passion rages through her body. She didn't want anything in her life she couldn't control or couldn't walk away from. She didn't want another failure. Not even in a sham marriage.

But what made his heart swell with pride and love was knowing she was trying to protect him from being hurt as well.

It had taken a great deal of courage to bare her soul to him, to confess her so-called failures. Obviously, she thought it would lessen her in his eyes. But it had only strengthened his feelings for her. *This* was the caring, compassionate, courageous woman that he had carried in his heart for so long. If it was within his power, he was going to take that haunted look from her eyes and show her the good things about herself she didn't see.

To accomplish that, he needed her to say yes to his proposal. He now realized he had gone about trying to convince her the wrong way. She was too stubborn and too wary of men to be pushed into a marriage that wasn't on her terms, but she could be *lured*. Thank goodness, he finally knew how to entice her. He was going to appeal to her greatest strength, her compassion for others. He only hoped he was a good enough actor to pull it off.

"I guess I came on pretty strong at times," Kane said mildly.

Her head lifted. "A little."

"Sorry, Tory. I guess after we kissed in the truck my brain went south." As Kane expected, Victoria ducked her head and began fiddling with the clasp of her purse again. "I can't believe I found someone to solve all my problems and I blew it."

Her head snapped up. "Problems?"

This time it was Kane who ducked his head. "I'm usually pretty self-sufficient, but lately I've gotten tired of going home to an empty house and eating meals alone." He sent Victoria a slanting glance. "If I go out with my married friends and their wives, I feel like a fifth wheel. Or I'm given the unwanted name of some woman their wives think would be perfect for me. If just the married guys and I go out, I have to listen to them talk about their wives. If I go out with my single friends, by the end of the evening they're ready to pick up anything breathing. I'm left alone again. That ever happen to you?"

Slowly she nodded. "I learned to take my car whenever I'm meeting single friends for dinner or drinks."

Kane's broad shoulders slumped as he crossed his arms and leaned against the counter top in the kitchen. "Then, there are the times when I stay home. I'm hungry, but nothing in the refrigerator appeals to me and even if I felt like driving, I don't know what it is I want to eat. Nothing on the TV is worth watching, and the book I wanted to read can't hold my interest past a couple of pages."

Kane sighed loud and eloquently. "I don't realize I'm lonely until the phone rings and I break my neck getting to it. Nine out of ten times it's a solicitor and it takes all my willpower not to hang up on them."

This time Victoria spoke without being prompted. "I guess most single people feel lonely once in a while."

"You been to your high school reunion yet?"

Victoria blinked at the seemingly arbitrary change of subject. "No."

Kane suspected Victoria probably thought bull-dogging the calf had rattled his brain. "Last year at my high school reunion, I was the only one out of my class of two hundred and seventy eight that hadn't married. Some were working on marriage number two or three." He shook his dark head. "I'm going to pass on going to my college reunion in July."

"Why?" Victoria asked, unwittingly walking right into Kane's trap.

"Everyone will be asking if I got married and I'll have to say no. I've already heard from a few of the guys. As soon as I tell them I'm single they start trying to match me up with someone." His gaze sought hers. He couldn't tell if she was swallowing his line or not. For good measure, he tried to make his voice sound as sad as he hoped his face looked. "You would have been perfect and saved me a lot of trouble. No one would have suspected that you were pretending to like this face of mine."

"There is nothing wrong with your face," Victoria snapped defensively.

He didn't smile, but his heart did. "After Bonnie explained your problem, I really started looking forward to going back to Prairie View. You would have been by my side, my arm around your waist, maybe a kiss or two."

Victoria bit her lip.

Kane wondered if he should have left the kissing out. No. She needed to know up front they were going to act like a happily married couple in public. He only hoped one day it wouldn't be acting.

"If we had gotten married it sure would have helped me out. You don't know how tired I get of the measuring looks from my friends when they talk about their wives and families. Even my mother has started giving me a hard time. I stopped telling her when I was coming home because I don't want to be cornered by some woman my mother thought would make me a good wife."

At least that was the truth. The last time he had gone to Tyler to visit his parents, not less than three women just happened to drop by. Any fool could have seen it was a setup. After the last one had gone, he warned his mother if she ever did that again, he would get in his truck and leave.

"She sounds like Grandmother," Victoria said.

Kane sighed. "She keeps telling me she wouldn't worry about me so much if I had a wife to take care of me. I can take care of myself, but it would be kind of nice having someone who worried about me if I was late coming home. Being married would have given me some breathing space with my mother and friends, a wife for the reunion, and someone to come home to."

Unfolding his arms, Kane pushed away from the counter. He wish he could tell if she was weakening. "We could have really helped each other out. I guess I better see you to your car."

He walked over to her, grasped her gently beneath the elbow and helped her to her feet. As soon as she was upright, he stepped back. "I'm sorry I blew things with you by coming on too strong. I'd ask for another chance, but I know how difficult it is for you to trust men."

"I trust you, Kane," she defended.

"Enough to give me a second chance?" he asked. The ringing silence and her downcast head was his answer. "I bet Matt wouldn't have any trouble finding a wife."

Her head snapped up. "He'd have even more trouble. Pretty men usually have pretty egos. You're kind and dependable."

"You just described a dog I once had."

She hit his chest with a closed fist. "Don't say that!"

His dark brows drew together. "Tory, you sure you feel all right? You want to lie down?"

"No, I don't." She took a deep breath, looked into Kane's eyes, which held so much concern for her, and knew what she had to do. "I hope you continue to be this solicitous about me after we're married."

He went still.

"We both have reasons for getting married. I don't see why we can't help each other." She wasn't going to find a better man than Kane to marry. She doubted if one existed. "Three months living together should be enough time to get your mother off your back and get you through your college reunion."

"Done," Kane blurted and extended his hand.

She lifted hers. "My grandmother and your mother will just have to be happy with a year of marriage."

He expected a lifetime with her. His hand closed over hers, his thumb stroked her skin. "You'll make a beautiful bride."

The velvet softness of his voice caressed her as much as his thumb did. Liking both too much, she quickly withdrew her hand. "My grandmother wants to meet you. The entire family will be there, but I don't want to mention our engagement. I couldn't stand all the questions."

His dark brow arched. "Are you sure that's the only reason?"

She frowned. "What other reason could there be?"

"I'll give you one guess," he answered with a wicked smile.

Her eyes blazed. "Will you give it a rest! If we're going to be married I can't be bothered watching every thing I say for fear you're going to take it the wrong way." Victoria gave him her grandmother's address. "Dinner is at seven. It's up to you if you want to come." The door shut with a decided snap behind her.

"Well, I'll be." Kane threw back his head and laughed. Victoria really knew how to dig her spurs into a man's hide. He rubbed his hand across his face. He had pushed too hard, but more than his next breath he wanted to see pride and love in her eyes when she looked at him. He should have known he'd be greedy where she was concerned.

After putting on one of Matt's shirts, Kane snatched up his misshapen hat, rammed it on his head and followed Victoria. He had a feeling this time she would wander the parking lots located around the stockyards all afternoon without coming back to ask him for help.

Kane caught up with her less than thirty feet away. "Promise me you'll put me in my place if I get out of line again."

The rigidness left her shoulders. She stopped and looked up at him. A shy smile curved her lips. "I will . . . if you promise to help me find my car."

"It's a deal, but there's one thing we forgot about our engagement."

"What?" she asked wearily.

"This." His head dipped, his lips took gentle possession of hers.

* * *

"Would you care for more apple pie, Kane?" asked Clair.

Swallowing the last bite of his second large slice, Kane shook his head. "No, thank you, ma'am."

Clair beamed at him, then at Victoria, as if they had given her something precious and rare.

Kane studied the petite yet regal older woman in ecru lace and pearls. Clair Benson wasn't what he had expected. She was charming and genuinely warm. She treated him like the proverbial prodigal son. Within two minutes of his and Victoria's arrival it was also obvious that his new fiancée was Clair's favorite among the fourteen other assorted relatives.

Despite their being late, Clair had insisted two chairs be brought into the living room so they could sit next to her. When they went in to dinner, Clair's husband escorted Victoria, and Kane took Clair's surprisingly firm arm.

"Do you come from a large family, Kane?"

"Grandmother, please. You've been quizzing him all evening," Victoria said.

"Kane doesn't mind. Do you, dear?"

Kane smiled. "I've got a feeling that whether I minded or not, you'd still want an answer."

"Age does have its privileges."

Victoria groaned.

"I'm the oldest of three children. The baby's a girl." Kane grinned. "But since she is about to get her chemical engineering degree from A&M, she doesn't want us calling her 'baby' any longer."

"I thought it was just you and Matt," Victoria said, before she thought.

"It never came up."

Victoria set back in her chair. It had never come up because she hadn't asked him anything, except how much money he wanted for his signature. "You must be proud of her."

"We all are."

"You should be." Clair nodded to Henry and rose. Everyone followed suit. "Victoria, take everyone into the living room. I'd like to show Kane something that I'm proud of."

"Grandmother, I—"

"I know you'd be happy to do it for me." Clair laid a hand on Kane's arm, then placed one on her husband's, who had come to her side. "We'll be in shortly."

Victoria heard the buzz of her relatives around her and knew they were speculating about her grandmother's attachment to Kane. If she wasn't so grateful that her grandparents had appeared to like Kane on sight, she might have balked. "Shall we go into the living room?"

* * *

"Wasn't she a beautiful baby? She's so special."

Kane looked at the black and white picture of the thin child who had her thumb in her mouth while holding the hem of her mother's flared skirt in the same hand. "I don't think we came in here to talk about Tory's childhood."

"Perceptive of you, young man," Henry said, looking over the wire rim of his glasses.

"Do you think a lesser man would have our Victoria in a dither?" Clair asked her husband.

"What did you say?" Kane asked.

"Don't go dumb on us now." Clair closed the oversized photo album. "What we'd like to know is why, since you and Victoria obviously care about each other, you had her so upset earlier today. If it's because you need money—"

Kane came to his feet. "I think I'd better go."

"Do sit down, Kane, and stop glowering at me, or Henry will have to take you to task," Clair said.

Kane glanced at Henry, who remained unmoved in his leather easy chair, his legs stretched out in front of him on a hassock, his hands folded across his lap.

"Please do as she asks or I'll have to defend her, and I don't relish any of my bones being broken, especially at my age," Henry said mildly.

"If we thought all you wanted was money,

we'd never let you through the door. We learned our mistake with Stephen," Clair said with heat.

"You should have protected her from that pile of—" Kane flushed and took his seat. "Sorry."

Clair patted Kane's hand. "I don't like to speak ill of others, but in Stephen's case, it's justified. It occurred to Henry and me that cattle ranching is a very unsteady business and you might be a little hesitant in asking for a woman's hand."

Kane almost relaxed at the antiquated term of asking a woman to marry you. "The ranch is solvent."

"Then there is no reason why you can't ask Victoria to marry you."

"That, Mrs. Benson, is between me and Tory."

"Did you know you're the only person she allows to call her anything besides Victoria?" Clair persisted. "There has to be a special reason."

"No, I didn't. As for a reason, I stopped trying to figure out why women did things before I got out of high school." He rose. "If you don't mind, I'd like to join the others."

Clair smiled indulgently. "I do believe you're as stubborn as I am."

"No," Kane said. "That dubious honor goes to Tory."

Chapter 7

The alarm clock's strident buzz woke Victoria. A groping hand shut off the intrusive noise. For the first time in days, worry hadn't prodded her from sleep and driven her from her bed long before the alarm sounded. It was all because of her engagement to Kane. He had given her back *Lavender and Lace*. In his giving, he had taken as well.

He had taken away her ability to group him with other men. He was Kane. Rugged, aggressive, yet so tender with her that she felt better just being around him. Rolling from her side, she lay back in bed staring at the gathered peach moire half-canopy overhead. What was there about Kane that slipped past her defenses, making her want to take the frown from his face? Whatever it was, she was going to remember they had a business arrangement and nothing else.

Throwing back the comforter, she got out of bed. Kane was picking her up around twelve to go get their marriage license, then they were going for lunch. Today he'd see a poised Victoria, not someone who shivered at his slightest touch. Today she would not spend her time wondering about a man who could be as rugged as a mountain or as gentle as the stream that wound through it.

However, once at *Lavender and Lace,* she continued to think about Kane. He clearly puzzled her. No one in the past had put her needs above theirs. Her parents had loved her, but she had understood from an early age that they had social and professional obligations to meet.

By forcing her into marriage in hopes of continuing the Chandler line, her grandmother put her own wishes above Victoria's.

Only Kane had put her first. He hadn't taken advantage of her moments of weakness in his arms or of her need for a husband. She paused in hanging up a slinky black chemise.

A man as giving as Kane deserved a woman who would cherish him as much as he would cherish the woman he loved. She would have to do a delicate balancing act of giving him a make-believe wife while not becoming too emotionally involved. Perhaps she should have said no kisses.

"I hope I'm not the cause of that frown?"

She pivoted. "Kane! What are you doing here so early?"

He stepped closer. Her body heated. "I needed something."

"W-what?"

A long, tapered finger traced her quivering lower lip. "Guess?"

Her throat dried. What must she have been thinking to agree to a public display of affection? Kane was too good at making a woman feel special and needed. "I can't leave the store now."

His black Stetson jerked in a clerk's direction. "Can't she take care of things?"

"Melody is very competent, but I usually help and it's almost time for her lunch break." Victoria stepped around him and away from temptation. This time when they talked, she was going to be sensible. No more kissing. "Melody," she said, going behind the solid oak counter. "You can go to lunch now."

Melody, petite, pretty, and a redhead for the past three days, glanced at Kane who leaned against the eighteenth century armoire, his arms folded as if he lounged daily in the midst of a lingerie shop. He tipped his hat, his dark gaze returning to a fidgeting Victoria.

"Is he yours?" Melody inquired.

Used to the young co-ed's direct way of speaking, Victoria simply gave her the answer she sought. "Yes."

"Does he have a brother?" Melody persisted, her voice carrying as she gave Kane a thorough once over.

Kane grinned. "One, and he's a lot harder to catch."

"Melody, you're wasting your lunch time." Victoria reminded her, then grimaced as she heard the irritation in her voice.

"Sorry, but it isn't often you see a man so well built. He's got some killer eyes, too. I'll just get my purse and leave." Retrieving her purse from the back, she did just that.

Kane pushed away from the armoire, his steps slow and predatory as he came to Victoria. Reaching over the counter top, he lifted her chin with finger and thumb. "Thank you."

"For what?"

"For pretending to be a little jealous."

"I don't know what you're talking about," she informed him, turning away.

"Oh, no you don't," Kane said, his incredibly gentle hands palmed her face. "I've seen compassion and desire in your eyes. Jealously, even pretending, is something I never hoped for, and you're not going to deny it."

"We *are* engaged," Victoria said, thankful he didn't realize she hadn't been acting. What had happened to her earlier plans to keep things on a business level?

"That we are." A rough-tipped thumb stroked the smooth line of her jaw. Her stomach somersaulted.

Her hands closed over his. "Kane, you can stop now. No one is in the shop."

"Yes there is." He inclined his head toward the front door.

Victoria snatched her hand away and quickly skirted the counter. She hadn't heard the bell. Thankfully, the young woman was a repeat customer and knew what she wanted. As soon as Victoria finished the sale, she returned to Kane.

"I think we sh—"

"How do you buy those things?" he interrupted.

Following his pointing finger, Victoria saw a reclining mannequin wearing a black lace merrywidow with plunging underwire cups. Garter straps hung down over a black G-string bikini and attached to lace-trimmed black stockings. "By sizes."

Kane looked at her, his eyes hovered briefly on

the rise and fall of her breasts beneath her yellow silk blouse, and he asked, "Sizes of what?"

Heat climbed from her breasts to her face. The twinkle in his eyes gave him away. "You should be ashamed of yourself."

"Didn't you know that when a man takes a wife he has no shame?" he asked softly.

"I-I'm beginning to."

"Finally, I'm getting somewhere. Now, wrap everything up," he ordered.

"You're serious?"

"I am." He leaned closer. "Maybe if I get lucky, I'll get to see my wife wearing them."

Excitement and uncertainty vied for her attention. Uncertainty won. "Kane, you shouldn't have to get lucky to see your wife wearing lingerie."

"Considering we're only pretending, I do," he teased. "But I am looking forward to sharing other things with you, like watching the sunset, having breakfast, going on a picnic."

"I haven't gone on a picnic since I was a little girl," Victoria said wistfully. "I bought a basket a while ago but I never got around to using it."

"You will now. I know the perfect spot." His fingertips gently touched her cheek. "You're going to knock the guys' socks off when we go to Prairie View for my college reunion. Now, let's see what else there is."

Taking her hand, he stopped in front of a red satin teddy. Fingering the lace at the bodice, he looked back at Victoria. His eyes narrowed. For a second his hand tightened on her arm, then loosened. He stepped away.

The front door bell sounded again. The customer and the one after her needed Victoria's assistance. Pointing to the front door, Kane mouthed "twelve" and left. Her gaze followed until the matronly lady asked Victoria about bath crystals in a tone that clearly stated she had asked the question before.

Showing the customer the different fragrances, Victoria glanced back at the closed door. Kane was apparently enjoying their engagement, but she was in deep trouble and sinking further each time he came near her.

Precisely at twelve, Kane returned. Victoria tilted her head toward the back office. Nodding, Kane walked in that direction. After she finished ringing up a sale, she followed.

"Business seems good," Kane said, looking around the room cluttered with several opened boxes.

Obtaining her purse, Victoria nodded. "This time of year is always busy with vacations and weddings." Her eyes slid away from Kane's.

His large hands spanned her waist, drawing her and her gaze to him. "You won't be sorry, and you'll never have to be afraid of saying no." His head bent, his warm breath flowed over her lips.

Victoria inhaled sharply and tasted something mint flavored. Instead of stepping back as she had intended, she licked her lips. Kane did the rest. Warm lips brushed against hers so fleetingly that Victoria's lashes barely settled against her cheek before they lifted again.

"If I kissed you the way I wanted, we'd miss lunch and I'd get into trouble for overstepping our bargain." Her hand in his, he started from the room. "Now, let's get going. We have a lot to do."

The phone rang just as they reached the door. Quirking a dark brow, Kane released her hand. "Make it quick or I might have to start nibbling on you."

Flushing, Victoria picked up the phone. She wondered if there would ever come a time when her body would be immune to Kane's teasing. She sincerely hoped so.

Her voice was breathless when she spoke, "*Lavender and Lace.*" Pause. "Hi, Bonnie. Yes, he's here." She handed Kane the phone. "She wants to talk with you."

"Hey, Bonnie, don't you get tired of bothering

us?" Kane spoke jokingly into the receiver. His smile abruptly faded. "Mama?"

His uncertain gaze flicked to Victoria. "Yes, ma'am, it's true."

A hard knot settled in Victoria's stomach. Instinctively, she stepped closer to Kane.

"Don't cry, Mama. I was going to call you." He paused. "Yes, I'm with her now. Addie? Sis, don't tell me you're on the line too. No, you can't have a discount, and get off the other phone. Now!" He rubbed his hand across his face. "Sure, Mama, you can talk . . ." He glanced heavenward. "She won't think you're strange for crying." There was another pause. "That sounds fine, Bonnie." His expression looked anything but fine. "All right, Mama. Good-bye."

Hanging up the phone, he leaned against the desk. "Since it's Friday, my sister came home from college for the weekend. She called Bonnie to thank her for her graduation gift, and Bonnie told Addie one of her brothers was getting married. She yelled out to Mama, who thought it was Matt. Bonnie finally explained that it was me. Then Bonnie hooked us up to a three-way call. I guess you heard the rest."

He rubbed the back of his neck. "I wanted my parents to hear about the wedding from me.

Mama was crying and talking about losing her firstborn."

"How did you plan to explain to them that a woman is using you to regain control of her business?"

"I'm a grown man, not some idealistic kid. I don't have to explain anything to my parents or anyone else," he said fiercely. "I run my own life and make my own decisions. I meant they deserved to hear about our engagement from me first. I'm getting as much out of this marriage as you are."

"I shouldn't have told Bonnie last night when she called," Victoria admitted ruefully.

"It's all right, but there's something else."

"Why do I have the feeling that I'm not going to be pleased?"

"The whole family is coming up tomorrow evening at six to meet you. Before they do, I think it's about time I showed you where I live."

Kane was in trouble.

He knew it the moment he drove across the cattle guard to his ranch. Victoria's entire body tensed on seeing the initials K and T on each of the ten-foot black iron gates. Gripping the truck's steering wheel, Kane continued the mile-long drive on the paved road to his house.

A winding stream meandered on his left. On his

right, red Herefords lolled beneath cedar and oak trees or at the salt block. The white-faced cows' mooing broke the silence of the countryside. Kane wished something would break the strained tension inside the truck.

He pulled up in front of his two-story frame house bordered by a bed of dark gold zinnias. Kane grimaced on seeing his quarterhorse, Shadow Walker, run to the corral fence and nicker in greeting.

Getting out of the truck, he walked around and opened Victoria's door. "Come on, I'll show you around."

Without a word, she complied. Deciding to save the house for last, Kane started toward the outer buildings. Victoria became stiffer as he pointed out the barn, the stable for his registered quarterhorses, the tractor and hay combine under the galvanized shed, the bunk house for the three full-time hired hands.

Finally they started back. The house, painted white and trimmed in blue with blue shutters, had a wraparound porch. Three large baskets of ferns and a porch swing shifted in the gentle spring breeze. Kane opened the front door and stepped aside for her to enter.

Gleaming oak hardwood floors stretched from the front room to the staircase and beyond to the glass-enclosed porch. Hundred-year-old oaks shaded the enormous back yard. His worried glance flickered around the large open room filled with overstuffed chairs and antique furniture he had rescued and lovingly restored. It wasn't classy like her home, but it had a casual comfort that he liked.

"Grandmother would love this room."

Kane let out a sigh of relief. At least she was talking to him. "I'm more concerned with what you think."

She swung around. "The two-car garage I saw in back. Would it happen to have a gray Mercedes in it?"

Kane's expression turned grim. "Yes."

"Is this the reason you didn't want the girls at The Cuttin' Inn talking to me alone?" Victoria asked.

"Partly," Kane answered truthfully. "You seemed to think money was the determining factor for us getting married. It never was for me. I thought it more important for us to like and trust each other than for you to know I didn't need your money."

"How many acres does this 'little place,' as you put it, have?"

"Tory—"

"How many?"

"Just under a thousand."

Her hazel eyes glittered. "You're rich!"

"Depends on your definition of rich," Kane said, trying to lighten the mood. At Victoria's continued glare, he explained further. "I grew up on a small farm on the outside of Tyler in East Texas. The football coach in high school thought I'd be perfect for the defensive line, but I kept tripping over my feet or someone else's."

"Kane, there is nothing remotely clumsy about you," Victoria said without thought. "You move with the self-assurance of a man who knows who he is and where he's going. You must have been going through an adolescent phase of awkwardness."

Kane smiled. Even being upset with him, Victoria rushed to his defense. But the resurgence of the glitter in her hazel eyes told him he wasn't off the hook. "Coach Phillips also happened to be my algebra teacher. He discovered that what I lacked on the football field, I made up for academically. He liked to dabble in the stock market and got me interested. By the time I went to Prairie View on a math scholarship, I was pretty good at it."

"What happened to get you from there to here?" Victoria asked, her body no longer rigid.

"Nothing, for a while. I got my MBA in banking and finance, went to work as a financial consultant for an investment firm, and kept in touch with Coach Phillips." Kane shrugged his broad shoulders. "While I made some good investments, I quickly learned the only way I was going to stop being nine-to-five was to get in on the ground floor of a company before it went public. I started saving so I'd be ready."

Admiration shone on Victoria's face as she leaned against an overstuffed chair and waited for Kane to finish.

"The chance came with a phone call from Coach Phillips four years after graduation. A small cosmetic company in Dallas specializing in moderately priced skin care and makeup products for African-American women was going under and looking for backers. I checked it out and quickly discovered the company also needed a strong marketing plan and sound financial management to survive. After getting good feedback from mother and some of her friends who tested the products, I knew my chance had finally come."

"I only knew I wanted to be my own boss. Luckily, I was friends with a savvy businesswoman who owned a specialty dress store. She gave me a lot of good advice," Victoria said.

"Why did you choose lingerie?"

"Women deserve to feel pampered and beautiful." Victoria folded her arms. "Nothing can do that more than having something soft and luxurious next to her skin."

Kane started to argue that the right man could make a woman feel the same way, but decided he'd do better to keep the conversation in relatively safe waters. "I told the owner I could save his company, but in return I wanted a twenty percent share and a voice in the operations."

Victoria rolled her eyes. "Why doesn't that surprise me?"

"If you don't believe in yourself, who will?" he asked pointedly. Victoria remained silent. "Anyway, my investment paid off. 'Cinnamon' is among the top cosmetics firms in the country. About two years ago, I decided it was time to cut back on the time spent with the company and enjoy life more. My partner and the original owner, William Conrad, thrives on the hassle of running a corporation almost as much as he enjoys being solely in charge. I enjoy the ranch. This way we both get what we want and I don't have to worry about the fluctuating price of beef."

"I've heard of your company. You should be very proud of yourself." She straightened and looked him squarely in the eye. "I only have one question left. Why did you want to marry *me*?"

Kane was in trouble again. He had to be very careful how he answered. "I told you why I wanted a wife."

She glanced around the antique-filled room

and shook her head. "Not all of it. I might have believed I was your last hope yesterday, but not after what you just told me and seeing this place. You wouldn't have had any problems getting a wife. Some women can be as heartless as men when it comes to being greedy. Why me?"

It was on the tip of Kane's tongue to blurt out everything until he realized Victoria wasn't ready for the truth. She might be attracted to him, but she was fighting it every step of the way. Nothing would make her run from him faster than telling her he loved her.

"Well?" she prompted uneasily. "And remember, you believe in honesty."

"Some of the women I've dated saw my money and not me. Others only wanted a good time. A few just wanted to get married to the first man they could drag to the altar," Kane said without bitterness. "I needed a woman I could trust. A woman who had as much at stake as I did."

Victoria nodded in understanding. "With me, you knew I stood to lose *Lavender and Lace* if anything went wrong."

He may not have been able to tell her he loved her, but he could tell her how special he thought she was. "With you I get a woman who is compassionate, kind, loyal and beautiful. If I prayed to God on bended knees for a thousand years,

I couldn't have gotten better. And . . ." His eyes twinkled. "You're really getting good at this pretend kissing stuff."

Her face softened moments before she tucked her head. "You shouldn't say things like that."

"I know, but it's such a pleasure to tease you and watch you blush. I never thought I'd find a woman like you. Maybe this will help you forgive me." Reaching into his shirt pocket, he withdrew a ring. At her continued silence, unease twisted through him. "Don't you like it?"

Victoria looked at the square-cut diamond surrounded by emeralds. The brilliant stones glowed with an inner fire reflecting the sunlight filtering through the large double windows behind her. "You're doing it again," she said, her voice barely audible.

"Doing what?" Kane frowned, clearly puzzled.

"Overdoing it. Giving and expecting me to take. Ours isn't a real engagement. I don't need a ring."

"I thought we settled this last night. To all outside appearances our marriage will be the real thing. Everyone who knows me would be suspicious if you didn't have a ring on." One long finger stroked her cheek. "Wear my ring, Tory."

"I can't," she said quietly. "You should save it for your real wife."

"Then I guess you better put this on, because

for the next year you're going to be my real wife," he said, picking up her left hand and sliding the ring on the third finger. He never planned for her to take it off.

"Will you listen to me," Victoria said, trying to free her hand. "I'm not wearing your ring."

"Wanna bet?"

"You're weak, Victoria. Weak. Weak," Victoria mumbled to herself as she walked out the leaded glass front door of her grandparents' house at ten minutes to six. Ruefully, she looked at the beautiful ring glittering on her left hand. She should have been stronger. But Kane had looked at her with those "killer eyes," as Melody had called them, stroked her with his velvet voice, and she'd forgotten about resisting.

For so long now she had prided herself on being her own woman, making her own decisions. Since Kane had entered her life, she didn't appear to be able to do either. Now, she faced the added responsibility of meeting his family.

Kane and his parents would be coming down the boxwood-edged driveway and pulling up within minutes. Brushing a hand over her beige linen suit, she shifted from one foot to the other. Her stomach had been in knots since leaving Kane's ranch the previous day.

On the return trip to town they decided the best thing to do was to stick as close to the truth as possible. A call to Bonnie confirmed that she hadn't told his mother where or how Victoria and Kane had met. Although Bonnie had an early-morning flight out of DFW Airport to New York for an art show, she promised to come and give moral support that evening.

A gray car appeared, followed by two trucks, one of them black. Kane opened his door first and started toward the car. A few feet behind him walked a stunning young woman with stylishly cut short black hair. She wore a cropped herring-bone jacket, a white blouse, and wide-legged black trousers.

Bonnie and her mother, Doris Fisher, emerged from the front seat of the car. Out of the back stepped a slender, gray-haired woman whose smile was slightly hesitant. Kane put his arm around her waist, then took the arm of the raw-boned man who had climbed down from the truck Matt drove. Releasing the older couple, Kane came to stand by Victoria.

"Mama, Daddy, Addie, I'd like you to meet Victoria Chandler, my fiancée."

Victoria extended her hand. "I'm pleased to meet you."

Mrs. Taggart's black eyes misted. "Kane, she's

beautiful. I always knew you'd choose someone extraordinary."

"Why should a son be any different from his father?" Mr. Taggart said, his gaze warm and loving on his wife.

"Hello, Victoria," Addie said. "He's the best there is, so treat him nice."

"Hey," Matt called as he walked up to the small group. "What about me?"

Addie snorted. "Why would any sensible woman marry you when she could have Kane?"

Matt smiled, and this time it almost reached his eyes. "I once knew a sensible woman who stood in front of a calf running for the exit gate in order to get a man's attention."

Victoria flushed.

"Don't mind Matt, Victoria," his mother said, giving her middle child a stern look. "We have so much to talk about. I want to know everything. Where and when you met? Why I'm the last to know?"

Victoria's smile slipped only for a second. "Please come inside. We'll talk there. My grandparents will want to meet you."

"They've already met Kane?" asked Mrs. Taggart crisply.

Victoria glanced at Kane. "He came to dinner the other night."

"They know about the engagement?" Censure laced Mrs. Taggart's voice.

Victoria and Kane exchanged another look. "We called them after Kane talked to you," Victoria said, glad to be able to tell the truth about something.

Mrs. Taggart's expression softened. "Then I wasn't the last to know."

"No, Mama, you weren't," Kane said. "But from what I know about Victoria's grandmother, she probably already has the wedding planned."

"I hope not," his mother said. "There are a few things I'd like to have a say about."

Kane and Victoria exchanged another look and groaned.

"The rose garden will be perfect for the wedding."

"All the Taggarts have been married in church."

"The colors will be pale pink and white."

"Peach would be prettier."

"She'll carry roses."

"Gardenias."

They agreed on nothing. Although Clair Benson and Grace Taggart sat close to each other, their ideas were light years apart. They had started planning "the children's wedding" five minutes after the introductions. Dinner and protests from

Victoria and Kane were seen as minor obstacles. To Victoria it was no wonder the men left as soon as they finished dessert.

Their excuse was to watch Matt in the calf-roping finals at the rodeo. The look of relief as they almost ran for the door told its own story. The Taggarts might be a rodeo family, but hers wasn't. Yet her own grandfather had supervised the fast exit. Bonnie, Doris, and Addie gave Victoria sympathetic glances and tried to remain out of the war zone.

Victoria kept her eyes on the sitting room door. One hour ticked into the next. How long did it take to rope a calf anyway? "Matt's best time is 5.3 seconds. The record is somewhere around 4.8 seconds."

Victoria's startled gaze swung to Addie, who had an impish smile on her beautiful almond-colored face. Realizing she had spoken aloud, Victoria glanced around.

"Pay attention, Victoria," admonished Clair. "It's nice to know you miss Kane, but we have work to do. You can't even decide on a simple thing like the flowers for your bouquet, let alone big decisions like china or crystal pattern."

Panic swept through Victoria. There was no way she was going through that again. "Grandmother, Mrs. Taggart, perhaps we can just spend the time getting to know each other and finalize the plans for a small wedding later."

"That's just it, Victoria," Mrs. Taggart chimed in. "We don't have the luxury of putting anything off. I can't believe Kane only gave you two weeks. You both deserve a proper wedding."

"As long as the minister pronounces us man and wife, it will be," Kane announced from the doorway.

"Kane!" Without thought, Victoria was on her feet and running to him. His arms closed around her waist and pulled her close. The comforting warmth of his body reassured her. She pressed even closer.

"That bad huh?" he asked gently, and smiled down into her upturned face.

The rumble of his deep voice vibrating through Victoria made her want to curl up in his lap. Her eyes widened with the realization of where her thoughts had strayed, what she was instinctively doing.

She tried to pull away. His arm became a steel trap. The smile on his face remained, but the eyes were unrelenting. She wasn't going anyplace.

"If anyone is interested, I came in second," Matt stated laconically.

"What stopped you from being first?" Addie asked.

"That's right, Kitten. Keep him humble," Mr. Taggart said as he and Henry brought up the rear.

Matt grunted and leaned against the door frame.

The Taggart family laughed. Victoria glanced around and again saw the family closeness. No one noticed that she had panicked. They were too involved in sharing Kane's illusion of happiness.

"Matt, you know I care, but at the moment we're trying to plan a wedding on an impossible schedule." Mrs. Taggart picked up a color chart. "Victoria has yet to pick out her colors."

"I don't know about hers, but mine is any color she's wearing," Kane said, a lazy smile on his dark face.

Warmth Victoria didn't want to feel, shouldn't feel, spread through her. Kane always said the right words. Why couldn't she do the same without getting restless? She pulled away and this time he let her go.

"I think we should have the reception with a sit-down dinner at the Four Seasons," Mrs. Taggart suggested.

Clair straightened in her seat. "Well, I don't. If the wedding can't be here, I insist the reception be held in the garden."

Mrs. Taggart shook her head. "You have a beautiful home and I'm sure the grounds are just as lovely, but ours is a big family, plus all of Kane's friends. If they can make it, I'd say we're looking at two hundred people easily."

Victoria's eyes widened. "You're planning on feeding over two hundred people at a sit-down dinner?"

"It will be our wedding gift to both of you. Thanks to Kane's financial advice, his father and I can afford to be generous," Grace said proudly.

"No." Victoria said. "It's too much. We're having a simple wedding. Isn't that right, Kane?"

"Whatever you say, Tory. Thank you, Mama, Mrs. Benson, but it's up to Tory. Go get your things, honey, and I'll follow you home."

"Kane, you can't take her home. We have too much to decide," Clair said, looking at Grace Taggart for support.

"Kane?" Grace said hesitantly.

"We're leaving," Kane said, a note of finality in his voice.

Grace leaned back in her seat. "I'm sorry, Clair. When he gets stubborn, there is nothing anyone can do to change his mind. Since his decisions are usually sound ones, the family learned to give in a long time ago." She sent her eldest a penetrating glare. "Now I'm beginning to wonder if that was such a good idea."

Kane grinned. "I love you too, Mama."

"I'm ready." Victoria reentered the room, her car keys in one hand and her purse in the other.

"Good night, everyone, and thank you for sharing tonight with us. Thank you for having us, Mr. and Mrs. Benson. Mama and Daddy, I'll call tomorrow." Kane brushed a kiss across his mother's cheek, then led Victoria to her car.

"Thanks for the rescue. I wasn't sure how much more I could take."

"It will be over soon."

"I may not last that long."

"Kane, Victoria. Wait a minute," Addie called as she ran down the walk to them. "Please don't kill the messenger, but both of you are expected back here after church tomorrow to continue discussing wedding plans."

Victoria looked at Kane. "We should have escaped while we had the chance."

Things are getting out of hand, Victoria thought as she drove to her apartment. Tomorrow, her grandmother and Kane's mother would politely ask Victoria and Kane their opinion, then do exactly as they wanted. Unfortunately, what they wanted was to turn a quiet ceremony into a social event.

A large wedding would only make things worse for her and Kane. Instead of acting like an ecstatic bride-to-be, she knew she would act the way she felt, scared and unsure of herself. Deceiving hundreds of guests would be next to impossible. She'd embarrass and humiliate Kane. She couldn't do that to him.

Another increasing concern was her growing attraction and dependence on Kane. His size and strength might once have intimidated her, but she was beginning to rely on that same size and strength. And reliance on a man, even one as nice as Kane, was sheer stupidity.

Neither of them spoke as they took the elevator to her floor. Inside her apartment, Kane said, "Sorry, Mama means well."

"Kane, I'm the one who should be apologizing." Victoria tossed her purse onto an easy chair. "Your mother is doing what any woman in her place would do. It's not her fault I'm a fraud."

"Tory, don't." He reached for her, but she moved away to pace the length of the fireplace.

"You should have heard her after you left. She was so pleased that some unscrupulous woman wasn't marrying you for your money." Shaking her head, she glanced away. "I can't go through the next thirteen days planning a big wedding I know is going to end in divorce."

"I'll have a talk with my mother."

"That still leaves my grandmother, and no one is going to keep her from doing what she wants."

He nodded. "What do you suggest?"

There was only one way out of this. "Do you have any objections to signing a premarital agreement tonight?"

His face remained impassive. "No. After what happened with Stephen and your grandmother, I didn't think my word would be enough."

Victoria winced on hearing the bleakness in his voice, but she couldn't turn back now. "I'll call my lawyers."

"Why won't it wait until tomorrow?"

"Because if you can possibly change your mind about a church wedding, I'd like to get married tonight."

Chapter 8

"We're home."

Shutting off the truck's ignition, Kane glanced at his bride. Nothing moved except her head as she looked at the dark house. She hadn't said a word since they walked out of the justice of the peace's home an hour ago. It was as if only then did the full magnitude of what they had done finally hit her. She was scared.

So was he.

Getting married had been the easy part. Signing the premarital agreement at her lawyer's house had taken less than thirty minutes. Tracking down a district judge who could waive the seventy-two-hour waiting period took a little longer, but less time than it would have taken for them to drive across the state line to Oklahoma.

Luckily, the judge's neighbor was a justice of the peace. Neither the JP nor his wife seemed the least bit bothered that he was being asked to marry someone at one o'clock in the morning. Nor was the JP concerned that he had to repeat the vows several times to the bride.

When he pronounced them man and wife, Kane had turned to kiss Victoria. He was unsurprised to see the fear in her drawn face, taste it in the coolness of her lips. He had a bride, but it remained to be seen if he had a wife.

Teaching her to love him was going to be the hardest and most important job he had ever undertaken. Yet, what if he couldn't get her to overcome her fears and learn to care for him? What if at the end of the three months she walked out of his life? Callused hands clamped on the steering wheel. That wouldn't . . . *couldn't* happen. Until tonight, each time she was with him she became less wary, more accepting of him, of his touch.

Until now. Now she was as wary of him as a chicken at a fox convention. He knew it would get a lot worse before it got better.

"I'll get your suitcase out of the back." He got out of the truck, relieved to hear the passenger door open and the glide of material across the leather seat.

Unlocking the front door of his house, he flicked

on the light. Her back ramrod straight, Victoria's heels clicked loudly on the hardwood floor as she walked into the living room. Woodenly, she faced him. Seeing the continued cautiousness in her large hazel eyes, he fought the growing urge to draw her into his arms and tell her he loved her.

Since nothing would send her running from the house faster, he pushed the words down inside his heart and hoped one day he'd be able to set them free. "Do you want me to put those papers in the safe?"

Her grip on the large manila envelope tightened. Her gaze lifted to his, then skittered away. "I . . . er . . . no."

"Tory, listen to me. I outweigh you by at least a hundred and twenty pounds and you're clutching a piece of paper that says we're man and wife." She flinched and he cursed under his breath. "I know you don't have a very good opinion of men, but you don't have to act as if we're on a deserted road and I've dragged you into the back seat of a car and you can't decide how far you want to go or if you should grab for the door handle and get the hell out of there. With me you'll always have a choice."

Her head snapped up. Kane met her gaze squarely. He saw her too clearly.

Women always talked about wanting an intuitive, sensitive man. Victoria doubted seriously if they knew what they were getting themselves into. What woman in her right mind wanted a man who could easily determine her mood, her thoughts?

A man who knew what you wanted before you did was bad enough, a man who looked into your heart and read your soul was lethal. Her ex-husband hadn't been nearly so perceptive and he had made her life a living hell. She turned away.

"Tory?"

Impatience. It vibrated through that one crisp word. Sometimes Kane wasn't a patient man. In her mind's eye she could see him standing behind her, hands on hips, his black eyes narrowed. If she didn't answer in his time frame, he'd touch her. Heaven help her, she liked being touched by him.

"If you can't find it in you to try and make this work, we're going to have the worst three months of our lives," Kane continued. "Despite your grandmother meaning well, she made you trust a little bit less. I'm willing to let you take your time, but you have to be willing to try."

Finally, she faced him. "What if I can't?"

Sadness swept across his rugged brown face. "I'm betting you can. I'm betting you're stronger than you know. I'm betting you'll remember you can trust me. A judge didn't have to tell me to honor and cherish you. Trust me, Tory. Trust yourself, because I don't think I can take you scurrying away from me or looking at me with fear in your eyes for the next three months."

Neither could she take the disheartened look in his face. Kane deserved better from life, from her. She just wasn't the woman to love him the way he deserved. Memories of her first marriage were too painful for her to want to remain in another one.

Tonight, standing before the justice of the peace, repeating her vows, had brought back all the foolish hopes she had during her first marriage ceremony. She hadn't known until her wedding night just how cruel and cunning Stephen was. Then it was too late. She was trapped by pride, by embarrassment, by her own foolish dreams.

Just like she was trapped in a marriage now to save her stores. She could only hope that she was a better judge of character than she had been ten years ago, and that Kane didn't change after he said "I do." In any case, she had to be as strong as he thought she was. "You better put these in the safe."

His face creased into a smile. "Come on, I'll show you the combination. Then we'll have a glass of champagne to celebrate the beginning of trust."

Kane's office was an interesting mixture of new and old. Worn blue leather armchairs, books, small western statues, and scattered rugs on the hardwood floor decorated the room. Bordered by two large windows was a massive desk with a computer and a printer on one end. In the far corner of the room sat an antique Wells, Fargo & Company safe that could have been used for an old western movie.

"You have got to be kidding."

"What other kind of safe would a real cowboy have?" He grinned boyishly. "It would take three strong men to lift it onto a dolly and ten sticks of dynamite to open this baby. Come on, I'll show you the combination so you can open it if you need the papers."

With only a moment's hesitation, Victoria knelt in front of the safe. Kane came down behind her. The heat of his powerful body wrapped around her as he reached past her to show her the combination. She had to concentrate to keep her hands from shaking as she repeated the maneuver. Three twists, a pull on the handle, and the heavy black door swung open.

Without a word, Kane handed her the manila envelope. She quickly placed it on top of a stack of papers, then swung the door shut. Warm fingers grasped her elbow and helped her to her feet.

"Let's go get the champagne out of the refrigerator."

"Do you always keep champagne chilled?" Victoria asked as she followed him into the blue and white kitchen. Obviously, Kane liked blue. She did too.

"A husband can't tell his wife all his secrets." Releasing her hand, Kane went to the refrigerator. "Grab a couple of glasses out of the cabinet."

Doing as he requested, she walked back to the round oak dining table for four. She glanced back to see Kane bent over, the snugness of his jeans over his hips. She jerked her gaze away from the oddly disturbing sight and looked around.

The kitchen was as spotless as the other rooms she had seen. She appreciated neatness, since she knew how much effort it took to achieve it. She disliked housework intensely. One of the first things she had done once her store began showing a decent profit was hire a housekeeper. What if he expected her to keep house?

"Here you go." Bubbling gold liquid filled her long-stemmed glass. Finished, he sat across from her as if realizing they both needed space.

"Your house is very neat," she ventured.

He cocked a dark brow. "Men aren't the slobs we're made out to be."

"I know that," she hastily said. "It's just that you didn't expect me, and yet the house is immaculate. That's more than I can say for my place."

"There wasn't a thing out of place when we went by your house tonight."

"Because I have a full-time housekeeper." Again she glanced around the kitchen with its glass-front white cabinets trimmed in blue.

"Tory, I didn't marry you to cook or clean house. I have a woman in twice a week to give the place a good cleaning." He studied the disappearing bubbles in the wine for a moment before meeting her eyes. "My father warned me it was easier to live with a happy woman than an unhappy one. Since most women like neatness, I never forgot it once I got a place of my own."

"Just your luck to get a woman who isn't neat," she bantered.

"There are other compensations," Kane said, his black eyes studying her closely.

The subtle shift in the conversation disturbed Victoria. "I think I'll go to bed."

He picked up his glass. "We haven't toasted yet."

Helplessly her gaze went to his strong hand gently holding the fragile stemware. After a moment, she raised her glass. "What do we toast to?"

"To lasting happiness and love," Kane said.

Victoria's delicate eyebrows lifted. After the horrors Stephen had put her through, she no longer believed in love and happiness.

"Tory," Kane prompted.

"To love and happiness." Victoria drank and allowed Kane to keep his illusions.

Draining his glass, Kane took both pieces of crystal and rinsed them in the sink. In the living room, he picked up her suitcase and started toward the stairs. "Willie keeps the room ready in case my family decides to spend the night."

"Is Willie the housekeeper?"

"Yes. Willimina Russell. She's been with me since I bought the place. She's always complaining about climbing the stairs. Now she won't have to."

Victoria pulled up short. "Why?"

Kane gave her an indulgent look. "Willie is almost as pushy as my mother. I'll see to our rooms. If she had any idea we weren't sleeping in the same bed, she'd ask questions."

"I can take care of my room," Victoria mumbled. The idea of Kane in her room, touching her things, was too intimate.

"She's also nosy." Kane's booted feet were muffled by the hooked rug running the length of the hallway. "I'll hang a few of your things in my closet and tell her you're using the connecting bedroom for your dressing room."

Something moved inside Victoria at the thought of her clothes hanging beside Kane's. Before she could analyze what, her mind scurried away. "You seem to have thought of everything."

"Not quite, but I'm working on it." Opening a door, he switched on a light.

Stepping inside the room, Victoria was instantly delighted with the white iron bedstead, washstand, and tri-fold mirror atop a double dresser. A nightstand by the bed held collections of miniature blue bottles and old Western photos of black cowboys.

"Is it all right?"

"It's wonderful," she said. "I've always liked antiques. It's as if you have a link with the past."

"I know." Brushing by her, he placed her luggage atop the bedspread.

"There are a lot of antiques in the house. Are you a collector?"

He shook his dark head. "No. I just like the idea of restoring old furniture no one wants and turning it into something beautiful and useful." He ran his hand lovingly across the washstand.

Victoria watched Kane's large hand stroke the oak wood and wondered if he thought of himself as something no one wanted. Sometimes she'd catch a glimpse of a vulnerable man; other times she didn't think a jackhammer would dent his hide.

"I have a friend in the antique business who keeps an eye out for pieces I might like. Some I can repair, but others . . ." He shrugged his broad shoulders.

Drawn by the soft lull of his voice, Victoria walked closer to him. "When do you find the time?"

"Nights mostly. Well, I guess I better let you get

some rest. The bathroom is through that door. The door next to it connects to my room. It doesn't have a lock unless you want one."

"No." She answered without hesitation.

The tightness in his brown face eased. "Good night, Mrs. Taggart." Warm lips brushed across hers. The door closed.

Fingertips pressed against her lips, Victoria stared at the door. She hadn't expected the kiss, but it hadn't annoyed her. Fact was, it had calmed her. No one had ever kissed her or treated her as tenderly as Kane. Best of all, he hadn't changed. Things were a little awkward between them, but nothing they couldn't work out.

Opening her suitcase, she picked up her nightgown. Light filtered through the wispy white cotton material. Fingering the spaghetti straps, she frowned. She didn't remember the gown being so revealing.

A noise lifted her head. She turned toward the floral covered wall she shared with Kane. It sounded like booted feet against a wooden floor. He must be getting ready for bed. She wondered if he slept in pajamas or nothing at all. Warmth spread through her. Her hand fisted. That kind of thinking would lead to trouble. In three months she planned to be back in her own apartment, in her own bed.

Going into the bathroom, she took a bath, then

slipped on her gown. Yawning, she turned back the covers and crawled beneath the cool sheets. Her hand was on the lamp's switch when she noticed the bouquet of red roses painted on the porcelain base.

Roses like the twelve individually wrapped ones Kane had insisted on buying from an all-night grocery store. He had arranged them into a bouquet and given them to her. "No bride should marry without flowers," he had said.

Instead of clinging to the roses, she had clung to the marriage license and the premarital agreement. Instead of berating her about being callous, he had asked her if she wanted the papers put in his safe. Instead of thinking about Kane's goodness, she had remembered Stephen's cruelty. Getting out of bed, she went downstairs.

He had fulfilled his end of the business arrangement; it was time she kept up her end. He wanted a woman who cared if he was late getting home. Such a woman wouldn't leave her bridal bouquet to wither. At the front door, she flipped on the porch light, then went outside to the truck. Opening the door, she leaned inside.

"What are you doing out here?"

In one motion she straightened and whirled. In her hand she clutched a long-stemmed red rose. A bare-chested Kane stood a few feet from her, his unsnapped jeans held up only by the flare of his hips. With difficulty, she pulled her gaze upward. "My flowers. I forgot."

Slowly his eyes moved to the rose, then to Victoria in her nightgown. He took in a deep breath, then let it out. A shudder of relief racked his body. She wasn't running away from him.

Listening to her leave her room and hearing the retreating footsteps panicked him as nothing else had. Finding her in his truck was almost unbearable. Seeing her sheer nightgown molded against her uptilted breasts and sleek curves wasn't any better. "Where are your shoes?"

She glanced at her feet, then at his. "Same place yours are, I'd imagine."

"My feet are a lot tougher than yours. Pick up your flowers and let's go."

"I hope you aren't going to be the dictatorial type of husband. You can't boss me around the way you did the owner of *Cinnamon*." Gathering the flowers, she closed the door. "Thank you for the roses. They're beau—"

Powerful arms picked up Victoria and held her against a muscular chest. Kane stared down at Victoria's lips, slightly parted and tempting.

"K-Kane, put me down!"

Since there was nervousness instead of panic in Victoria's voice, Kane ignored her command.

Slowly his gaze moved to her watchful eyes. He gathered her closer. He remembered the same cautious look when he had first held her twelve years ago. Then it had been the threat of a thunderstorm; now it was the threat of a husband.

"Kane, put me down," she repeated, her voice suddenly husky.

"Once we're inside." Kane started for the house. He tried to ignore the fullness of her breasts, the heat of her body through the sheer gown. "Besides, it gives me another chance to carry my bride over the threshold. Earlier you might have given me a black eye."

She heard the teasing note in Kane's voice and reacted to it, not the pounding of her heart. "Not if I didn't want a broken hand. I'll have to think of something more subtle if I'm displeased with you."

He laughed, a deep, booming sound, and gathered her closer. Victoria felt the heat and hardness of his body, tried to remain impassive in his arms, and lost the battle before he had taken another step. One arm inched around his neck.

Inside, he continued across the room and up the stairs. In front of her door, he released her so slowly that she slid against his body. A firm hand kept her there, his other hand brushed back her hair. For a long moment, he stared at her lips. "You better start thinking of my punishment."

His lips touched her, gently, then with growing hunger and need. His hands searched her body in a restless assurance, then settled on her hips to fit her lower body against his growing desire. With a small moan her fingers opened. Her hands slid around his neck.

Abruptly he tore his lips away. He pulled her arms from around his neck and stepped back. "Sorry. You make a man forget."

Dazed hazel eyes blinked open.

"I hope you won't hold this against me," Kane rasped.

"I—I No." Fumbling for the doorknob behind her, she finally grasped it, opened the door, and went inside.

Closing his eyes, Kane leaned his head back and drew in a deep shuddering breath. What had started out as a good-night kiss had exploded into something wild and untamed. He hadn't expected her eager response in his arms, and he sure hadn't expected his mind to whisper they were married and she was willing. He had almost lost it.

He knew he had made the right decision to make light of the kiss, but his body was paying the price. He wanted Victoria so much he ached. But he wanted a lifetime, not a night, and that was all he'd get if he made love to her now.

Knowing sleep was impossible and that nothing short of a tornado was going to get Victoria out of her room before morning, he went to his room to get dressed. He was going to his workshop.

He enjoyed working with his hands. The first piece he restored had been a chifforobe given to him by his maternal grandmother. It had taken him two weeks to get the old coats of paint off. He quickly discovered he liked seeing the worn, rough surface change before his eyes into a hidden treasure.

Victoria was another hidden treasure. To the casual observer, she was beautiful and untouchable. But if a man took the time to get past her defenses, he'd discover a vulnerable and sensitive woman who wanted to love and be loved. He was determined to be that man. If his plans went well, he'd finally put to use the small piece of furniture his mother had insisted on giving him after he bought the ranch.

He rubbed his broad jaw. Too bad he couldn't use sandpaper and varnish on himself. Passing Victoria's door, he stepped on something.

Roses were scattered around his feet. Bending, he picked them up.

Hope stirred.

He realized something he had initially been too scared, then too aroused to fully understand. Victoria cared enough about him to go outside and get her flowers. She hadn't even taken the time to put her shoes or robe on.

Whether she knew it or not, she was weakening. A smile lifted the corner of his mustache. He didn't need varnish or sandpaper. Just a sassy, sexy lady named Victoria Taggart. Pushing to his feet, he went to get a vase.

I can't hide in this room all morning. It's after nine. So I was in my nightgown clinging to Kane like lint to a sweater. He is my husband. So I'm attracted to him. Anyone can have a weak moment. At least the morning after my second marriage I'm not crying my eyes out the way I did after my first marriage.

Victoria had been arguing with herself all morning and had yet to come up with the courage to face Kane. She brushed aside the ruffled curtain to stare out the window. Brownish-green pastures and rolling hills spread out before her. In the foreground were the buildings Kane had pointed out days before. An hour ago she watched a thin, wiry man tramp back and forth between the stable and the bunk house, but nothing since then.

She still didn't understand why when Kane

touched her, her brain shut down and her body went into overdrive. Before now, memories of how Stephen had deceived, then almost destroyed her, had enabled her to remain emotionally detached from men.

Until Kane.

Well, that was about to end. Her chin lifted. She would not allow him to mess up her life. And she wasn't going to stay in her room all day. Walking to the door, she yanked it open.

Kane, his rugged face impersonal, filled the doorway. He lowered his balled fist. "How long had you planned on staying up here?"

"I was on my way down," she answered.

"Good, I need some company." Taking her by the arm, he took her to the kitchen. "Have a seat and help yourself."

The first thing she saw was the roses. Their long stems had been cut and they were in a short, wide-mouthed vase. Her fingers touched a dark red petal. A sensitive man like Kane could get a woman into a lot of trouble.

A large platter plopped on the table in front of her. Her mouth gaped. The blue stoneware overflowed with bacon, sausage patties, ham, French toast, scrambled eggs, biscuits, hash browns. "Who is going to eat all this?" She sank into her chair.

"I plan to give it a good try." Kane helped himself to a bit of everything.

"Do you always cook this much?"

"This morning I got carried away," he admitted. "I didn't know what you liked. Do you want coffee?"

"No. Juice is fine." She picked up her glass.

"After breakfast I'll introduce you to the hands."

"They're going to be surprised you have a wife." She sipped her juice.

"So are your friends." He looked at her empty plate. "Why aren't you eating?"

"I usually don't eat breakfast."

"You do now." He put two sausage patties, hash browns, and eggs on her plate.

Victoria folded her arms. "Didn't I warn you about being dictatorial?"

"Yes, but I'm willing to take a chance. Eat up. We have to go into town and tell our families."

"They aren't going to be happy," Victoria said, and picked up a fork.

"That's their problem." Kane's gaze fixed on Victoria's face. "But I'm going to enjoy every second of the time we have together. How about you?"

Chapter 9

The alternate knocking on the door and the ringing of the doorbell came as a welcome diversion for Victoria. "I think someone is anxious to see you."

Getting up from the dining table, Kane brushed aside the ruffled white curtain. "They're anxious all right. For both of us. It's my folks and yours."

"What?" Victoria rushed to the window. Two cars were parked behind Kane's truck. She didn't know about the blue car, but the burgundy one belonged to her grandparents. She might not be able to find her own car, but the fins and oversized headlights on her grandparents' '52 Cadillac were unmistakable. "How did they know?"

"Only one way to find out." Letting the curtain

fall, he started for the front room. With each step the noise at the front door become more pronounced. A few feet away, Kane glanced over his shoulder at Victoria. The corner of his mustache tilted upward. "Well, partner, do we slip out the back or face the angry mob?"

Despite her uneasiness, Victoria smiled. "Why bother? The back door is probably guarded."

"Victoria, I know you're in there."

"Kane, open this door."

Ignoring the demands of Clair Benson and his mother, Kane came back to Victoria. His hands settled on her shoulders. "I don't know about Mrs. Benson, but Mama blows out of steam quickly once she's spoken her mind. Everything will be all right." After a light squeeze of reassurance, Kane went to unlock the front door. The Taggart and Benson family were crowded on the porch. Only Addie and Matt were smiling.

Grace glared at her eldest. "Kane, I can't believe you were so irresponsible. I'd already called Pastor Hill."

Clair, her face pinched in disapproval, went straight to her granddaughter. "How could you do this to me?"

Before Victoria could answer, Kane placed himself between Clair and his wife. "There's no need to bully Tory."

Clair's brown eyes widened. "Get out of my way. Victoria is my grandchild."

"She's my wife."

One bony finger jabbed Kane's chest. "Sneaking around and getting married is nothing to be proud of. How do you think I felt learning my only grandchild eloped? And in the middle of early morning church service of all places! The judge's wife just leaned over and told me. I thought she was playing until she mentioned your name. I can only be thankful she didn't blurt it out."

"It seems to me that you should be congratulating us instead of being angry," Kane pointed out.

"No one has *ever* eloped in *our* family." Clair glanced around for her husband. "Henry, kindly move Kane out of my way."

From behind her came a groan and a chuckle. Kane knew Henry must be thinking of broken bones and Matt was enjoying the whole thing.

"Now, everyone. Calm down," Mr. Taggart said. "Kane is right."

"I think so, too." Addie smiled devilishly. "By the way, Victoria, I don't want to appear greedy, but how much of a discount do you give family members?"

"Addie, that's enough," Mrs. Taggart warned. "Your brother has acted totally irresponsible."

"It's not Kane's fault. I'm the one who asked him

to get married last night," Victoria said and moved in front of her husband. Every pair of eyes in the room converged on her. Silence reigned. Her chin lifted. "If you want to blame someone, blame me."

"You only had to ask once." Kane's strong arm circled her waist. "Mama, Mrs. Benson, we're sorry if you're upset, but Tory and I are responsible adults. The choice was *ours*. If anything, our marriage does credit to the way you raised us. We needed to be together and we wanted it to be right. I'm sure both of you can remember when you couldn't spend another minute apart."

For a charged moment both women stared at the newlyweds. Then with cries of happiness, the elderly women threw their arms around Victoria and Kane.

"Kane, I'm sorry."

"Victoria, forgive me."

"Come on, Grace and Mrs. Benson," Kane's father said. "Let's have a little feeling for the newlyweds and get out of here."

Grace and Clair sent Bill Taggart a hard glare, which he ignored. "Congratulations, son. Welcome to the family, Victoria." Mr. Taggart exchanged a masculine hug with Kane and kissed his new daughter-in-law on the cheek. "Henry, if you'll grab your wife, I'll get mine."

Henry did as requested, but not before he

shook Kane's hand and kissed his granddaughter. Smiling broadly, Addie hugged and kissed both the newlyweds. Matt winked at Kane and tipped his hat to Victoria. The door closed behind them.

"You were very convincing," Victoria said. If she hadn't known better, she would have believed his touching speech just as their relatives had. It annoyed her that she could still be so easily duped by a man.

"Was I? Come on and let's finish breakfast, then we can go pick up the rest of your things."

"There's no hurry. I thought I'd pick them up as I needed them."

"Well, think again," Kane told her. "Only a fool would believe our marriage is on the level if you go by your old place every day to pick up clothes. You'll have to find another excuse for staying away from me."

"That was not my intention," she flared. "You have no right to say such a thing."

"Saying what I want is about the only right I have with you and I'm going to do it whenever I please." He took her by the arm and started for the kitchen. "Our breakfast is getting cold."

Resisting the childish impulse to dig in her heels, Victoria decided to show her displeasure in another way. "I'm not hungry."

"Suit yourself. You can watch me eat."

* * *

Kane is a mean, spiteful man.

Snatching a sleeveless blouse from her closet, Victoria tossed it in the direction of the overflowing suitcase on the bed. He had to know she was hungry. It was after three in the afternoon. They had already made one trip back to his ranch with her car and a load of clothes, then returned for the second haul.

But had he asked if she was tired or hungry? No. And she wasn't going to give him the satisfaction of asking him to stop and eat. Of course he wasn't hungry after the huge breakfast he had put away. He lounged against her dresser, watching her pack as if he hadn't a care in the world.

Her stomach growled again. Her teeth gritted. "You have any clothes sturdier than these?"

Victoria glanced over her shoulder to see that Kane had finally moved. Hands on his hips, he stood by her bed, frowning down at the array of cotton, rayon, and silk blends scattered across the bed. All of them light and airy for the hot Texas summers. "They suit me," she said coolly.

Midnight black eyes swept upward. "Not on a ranch they won't. I don't want to hear you complaining if something gets caught on a nail or you get a splinter in your rear because you leaned against a piece of rough wood."

She clenched her teeth so hard her head hurt. "I promise I won't complain, but since you're so concerned, I'll confine myself to the house."

"No you won't. I want you with me."

"I've had enough of you. You've been bullying me ever since breakfast. It's about time you learned I push back. I'll wear what I want, when I want, and it's none of your business. If you want a constant companion, that's your problem."

"Are you finished?"

He looked mean and hard, but at the moment she didn't care. "For now."

He hugged her. "I knew you could fight back if I pushed hard enough."

She blinked, bemused by the hug and his statement. "You wanted me to get angry?"

"Not exactly. I just don't want you to be afraid to tell me off." He smiled. "I'm not always sure I'll listen, but you can try. How about on the way back we stop and eat?"

"You knew I was hungry?"

"Your stomach was growling so loud it shook the truck."

She punched him on the shoulder. "I'll get you for this."

"You can try."

They stood smiling at each other, until slowly their smiles faded. Her heart rate sped up. He looked at her lips. She looked at his.

He stepped back. For a moment she thought she saw regret in his eyes, then it was gone. His fingers uncurled from her waist. "We better get a move on."

"I suppose so," Victoria mumbled, feeling bereft and not understanding why.

"You want to wait or find someplace else to eat?"

Victoria glanced around the packed parking lot. There wasn't a space left. When Kane had driven by the front entrance of the popular seafood restaurant, she had seen people crowded against the stained glass door.

"Since it's Sunday afternoon, it's probably going to be the same everywhere," she told him. "Besides, I love the food here."

"That settles it then. You go inside and get our names on the waiting list. I'll stay here until I can park the truck." Kane pulled over to let a car pass. "Don't worry about your suitcases, I'll put them in front."

"Kane, that's a lot of trouble. We could eat someplace else."

"We could, but we aren't going to."

Victoria smiled. "Since my mouth is practically watering for some fried shrimp, I'll let you get away with being dictatorial this time." Getting out of the truck, she began to weave her way through the cars. She and Kane were really going to have to talk about his attitude.

"Victoria."

Shock ripped through her. Every nerve in her body went on alert on hearing the unmistakable sound of her ex-husband's voice. For a confused moment, she didn't know whether to continue to the restaurant or find Kane and leave. Remembering Stephen Malone's cruel streak, she decided against both. She turned.

Smiling as if he owned the world and everything in it, Stephen approached her. Rage built inside her against the man whose greed had nearly destroyed her.

No matter how she tried to feel relief that he was out of her life, anger always twisted and shimmered through her.

It always would.

Seeing her former husband was a harsh reminder of how pathetic and malleable and stupid she had been. In him, all her failures were magnified a thousandfold.

Stopping in front of her, his smile broadened. Dimples winked in his nut-brown face. "You're looking beautiful, Victoria, but then you always do."

"What do you want?" Victoria asked, her voice as chilling as the look she turned on him.

His smile faded. Nervously, he fingered the tan silk square in the breast pocket of his wheat-colored sport coat. "There is no reason why we can't be friends."

She laughed in his face. "I could give you a long list, starting with a hundred and ten thousand dollars. Do you want more?"

"Can't a man be forgiven for his mistakes?" he asked, a pleading note in his voice as he reached out to touch her arm.

A hard glare from Victoria stopped him inches from his goal. "Why this sudden interest in me?"

"Frankly, I've never gotten over you. Only I didn't realize it until recently. Richard saw you with a giant of a man at Wellington's last week and when he told me, it made me jealous. Today I was coming to see you and saw the same guy Richard must have been talking about help you into a truck at your apartment. On a hunch you were going out to eat, I followed," he explained, obviously proud he had been correct. "I've asked around and know you haven't dated much since our divorce. You must still care for me. Baby, I've never gotten over you either."

For a moment she was speechless. Of all the egotistical jerks! "You think I haven't dated because I wasn't able to get over you?"

Stephen's smile showed perfect white teeth and supreme confidence. "There's no reason for you to settle for such a mean-looking man. I know how insecure you are. I'm willing to take you back and we can start over."

"*I* wouldn't take *you* back if you were gold plated and had an apple stuck between those caps I paid for," she said furiously. "I didn't *settle* for less, I was lucky enough to get more. You are the one who is mean and cruel. My husband is more of a man than you could ever be."

Shock widened his eyes. "You married him!"

"Don't ever try to contact me again," she said tightly. "I know you lost your job and you need another meal ticket. This time, it won't be me."

Something cold flashed in his eyes. "Still trying to act more than you are just because you come from a wealthy family. You're no better than anyone else. How much are you paying him to tolerate a cold, shrewish woman like you?"

She flinched; he smiled.

"How does it feel knowing you're nothing but a beautiful shell?" he continued with malice. "A man might look at you, but your money is the only reason he'll stick around."

"You bastard!" Untamed fury swept through Kane. Before Stephen could move, Kane grabbed the smaller man by his throat and shook. Stephen's eyes bulged as he gasped for air.

"Tory is my wife and what's mine I protect. I never want to hear of you or see you within a hundred yards of her. Do I make myself clear?"

Gasping for air, Stephen clawed at Kane's unrelenting fingers. Kane's hand tightened. Stephen nodded. Kane unclamped his fingers. Stephen crumpled to the pavement.

Kane waited until Stephen looked up. Kane's smile was feral. "Stay out my wife's way. You'll be healthier. Now be smarter than you look and get out of here. Don't let me see you again."

Nodding, Stephen dragged himself to his feet with the help of a car bumper and staggered away.

Kane whirled to see several people watching him. Victoria wasn't among them. Brushing past the bystanders, he caught up with her and led her to his truck. He had rushed to her side as soon as he recognized the man Victoria had stopped to talk with. Kane closed her door. Victoria jumped. He hadn't been in time. Quickly, he got in on the other side.

"Tory."

"I was such a fool." Her voice trembled.

Kane's hand, reaching toward her, halted in

midair. His eyes shut. A hellish agony twisted through him. "Don't listen to him. He's a sorry bastard who wants to hurt you any way he can."

She looked at him with dark, pain-filled eyes. "I'm not hungry. Can we please leave?"

Kane's hand fisted. She was in pain and shutting him out again. He started the engine. He'd wait until they were home to finish talking to her.

But talk she would. That was her problem now—she kept too many things inside. He only hoped when she started talking, she wouldn't say something neither one of them could forget or forgive.

"Tory, I'm back with dinner." Kane sighed and knocked on the bedroom door again. He knew she was in there. Once they returned home, she had gone straight to her room. When he followed with her luggage, she hadn't acknowledged him in any way. Not even when he told her he was going to pick up something to eat.

Stopping at another restaurant was out of the question. From the shattered look on her face, he would have had to forcibly take her inside. She was hurt and angry. Unfortunately her anger was directed at herself and the closest man in her life. Kane.

He opened the door. She turned sharply away

from the window. Despite the anger emanating from her, he walked further into the room. "Dinner is ready."

She looked back out the window. "Close the door on your way out."

"I will, but you're coming with me. Walking or over my shoulder. Your choice."

Her shoulders jerked. For a charged moment he wondered if he had pushed her too far. Giving him a look that would have made a lesser man run, she stalked from the room. Kane followed.

Two feet inside the kitchen, she halted. Knowing the reason, Kane stepped around her and began opening the seven Styrofoam servers stretched across the blue counter top. "I didn't know what you liked, so I got a little bit of everything. Catfish, shrimp, crab cakes, flounder, french fries, hush puppies, and several different kinds of salad."

As he opened the last container, he glanced up. She had moved closer to the food. Her gaze was fixed on the batter-dipped butterfly shrimp. He snagged two plates from the table, handed her one and began to fill his own. The last thing she needed was him watching her. Finished, he sat his plate on the table and got a pitcher of tea and a diet cola from the refrigerator.

He joined her at the table, glad to see she had

put a decent amount of food on her plate. Without asking her anything, he opened the soft drink and poured it over a glass of ice. Head bowed, he said grace and heard her faint "Amen."

Kane ate with an eye on Victoria's plate. He made sure he kept it full. When he tried to give her the last fried shrimp, she shook her head. "Please, I'm stuffed."

"What about some pecan pie for dessert?"

"I'm too full to lift a fork, let alone have the energy to chew."

"Good. You sit there and I'll clean this up." Going to the refrigerator, Kane crouched down and began rearranging the food on the shelves. As he moved to get up, he saw Victoria standing with the containers in her hands.

"Working together, we can finish sooner," she said simply. She had wanted to hold onto her anger, to nourish it, stoke it against becoming vulnerable again. Kane's thoughtfulness had snuffed it out. Kane wasn't Stephen. He wouldn't hurt or use her.

"Thanks." He put the food away and stood up. "How about a walk to make room for the pecan pie?"

She lifted a brow. "I must be hearing things. You're actually asking?"

His mouth quirked. "I admit I'm a bit bossy. If you go with me, I'll try to mend my ways."

"Somehow I doubt you will."

"This is my favorite place," Kane said, spreading a blanket beneath a gnarled oak tree on a high hill overlooking his house. The ranch sat in a valley below, shedding its winter brown for spring green. Two horses played in the corral. Cows grazed a hundred yards away. "When the former owner brought me up here and I looked around and couldn't see another building, I knew I'd found my home."

Victoria carefully sat on the far corner of the blue blanket. "How long ago was that?"

He looked down at her before answering. "Eight years ago last month." Her body tensed again. He had bought the place two weeks after her divorce was final.

"You never looked back?"

"I made mistakes, if that's what you mean."

"None like mine." Self-reproach rang in her voice.

"It's time you stopped blaming yourself." He dropped down to his knees. "You're afraid you'll make the same mistake in judgment. Afraid you'll trust the wrong man again."

The truth of his words took her by surprise. Intuitive and dangerous.

"Do you think I'd use you?" he asked softly.

She had no defense against the need in his beautiful black eyes. "No. You're not like Stephen. I looked at him, really looked at him today, and couldn't believe I was ever fooled for a moment by his so-called charm and good looks. He used me, and I was stupid enough to let him."

With all his heart Kane wanted to take her into his arms, but if he did, she might stop talking. She needed to be able to put Stephen behind her, to know trusting him hadn't made her a lesser person. "You were young and impressionable. Blame Stephen, not yourself."

Her arms wrapped around her updrawn knees, she rocked back and forth and remembered. Stephen's attitude changed toward her the moment they boarded the cruise ship for their honeymoon. The gentle, considerate man she had fallen in love with was replaced by an argumentative, abusive stranger. The steward had barely closed the door to their cabin before Stephen pulled her down on the bed. He said he couldn't wait to make love.

She quickly learned the rough sexual act that followed had nothing to do with love. Stephen didn't care that it was her first time or that she was scared and unsure of herself. He wanted her and he had taken what he wanted. Afterward she lay crying as he hurled insults. He said it was her fault he had finished so quickly. He thought he had married a woman, not a cry baby. Without asking, he had taken some money from her purse and slammed out of the door saying, "At least I can have a good time in the casino."

Victoria shook her head, sending her black hair dancing around her tense shoulders, trying to stop the memories, but it was useless. Stephen had returned to their cabin hours later and apologized. The captain of the vessel had asked about her and wanted them to sit at his table. Excited about the honor, Stephen had promised not to resume their "lovemaking" until they were home. Once again, he became the old Stephen. At the time, she was naive enough to think he was concerned for her instead of concerned about presenting a picture of a devoted husband and happy wife.

His changed behavior made her think he might be right about things being her fault. After all, she had failed so many times in the past. Perhaps she just wasn't a sexual person. Once home, she had tried to make up for her deficiency by giving in to his demands of moving to a high-rise condominium, and letting a design studio do all the decorating.

A month after they were married, he wanted her to co-sign a loan for a new sports car. Neither one of them had a job and they both already had good cars. She refused. That night she had to endure his sexual demands for the first time since their honeymoon. The next day, she signed the papers. She learned to loathe Stephen, sex, and herself. But she learned the power of money over a greedy man.

"The things I let him say to me, all the humiliation I suffered at home and in public. The countless times I gladly came home knowing he was being unfaithful and not caring. I only cared that I wouldn't have to be bothered by a man whose touch sickened me. When there were no other women, I used his greed to keep him away from me."

Something clicked in Kane's mind. "You paid him to keep out of your bed, didn't you?"

Chapter 10

Her eyes widened on realizing what she had unintentionally admitted. No one knew that awful secret, not even Bonnie. With a strangled cry, she tried to get up.

Kane caught her. Ignoring her fists, he pulled her into his arms and down onto his lap. "It's all right, Tory. It's all right. You did the only thing you could think of."

Shame swept through her. "Let me go."

"No. Maybe this will convince you he was wrong." His lips sought hers.

Victoria turned her head and clamped her mouth shut. Kane veered to her throat and kissed the cord of her neck. He nuzzled the curve of her jaw, then ran the tip of his tongue across the seam of her closed mouth. With a delicate shudder, she opened for him.

Kane rewarded her by cherishing what she offered. He kissed her with all the tenderness and need he had held within him for so long. His tongue dipped and swirled, stroking the smooth inside of her mouth, the delicious heat of her tongue.

A long time later he lifted his head. He stared down at her tangled hair he had lovingly mussed, her dazed eyes, her lips moist and swollen from his kisses. With knives cutting through him, he waited until her gaze cleared and she focused on him.

"I'm not Stephen. Don't ever confuse us." His breathing ragged, Kane rolled away and stood. They both needed the space. "It's not your fault Stephen's a bastard." For a long moment he let the words lay between them.

"Don't you understand? There's not a cold bone in your body. He didn't know how to appreciate what he had. It wasn't your fault." At her continued silence, he reached for his waning control and sat down on the blanket again.

"You're a beautiful, sensual woman. He tried to make you less because that was the only way he could control you. Don't let him win. Put the blame where it belongs and get on with your life. Stop looking for him in other men. In me."

Mutely she stared at him, then looked away. "I'd like to go back, please."

Her voice was polite and correct and distant. Kane wanted to smash something. Instead he grabbed a fistful of blanket as soon as she stood.

Victoria looked at Kane's rigid profile. Misery twisted inside her. She didn't want to have her emotions probed. She wanted to be left alone. Even as the thought ran through her mind, she knew she lied. That was the reason Kane frightened her as much as his kisses thrilled her—She wanted to open up to him.

Yet she knew if she forgot the painful lesson Stephen taught her, and yielded to Kane, he would touch her in ways Stephen never had, leaving her exposed and defenseless. This time, if something were to go wrong, she wasn't sure if she would heal again.

He grabbed her arm and started down the hill. "Let's go. But we're not finished with this."

"Why do you keep pushing me to talk about him?"

Kane stopped and faced her. "Because you're my wife, and even pretending, I don't like the idea of your ex-husband having any influence over you."

Mixed feelings surged through her. "I don't want to be vulnerable again."

"No one does." His voice softened. "Just take the first step. I'll be with you all the way."

She bit her lower lip. "I may try your patience."

"You already have," he stated bluntly. "But we're a team now. We have to work together." He started walking again. "Can you play dominoes?"

Victoria thankfully grasped for the change of subject. "Grandfather says I can."

"After we get your things unpacked, we'll find out."

Her arms crossed, Victoria watched Kane put the dominoes back into the box. "You cheated," she said with a pout.

Kane never looked up. "You're such a lousy player, I didn't have to."

Victoria leaned over the table and punched Kane on the arm. "I am not. Grandfather and I played all the time and I seldom lost."

"Knowing what a poor loser you are, he probably let you win to keep the peace," Kane said. He rose and put the dominoes back on the bookshelf.

Victoria pursed her lips. "Maybe. I hate to lose."

"That's what your grandmother was counting on."

Her playful mood evaporated. "I guess so."

"You're going to have to stop doing that."

"Doing what?"

"Withdrawing each time the reason we got married comes up."

She sighed. "I'm working on it."

"Good." Walking over, he pulled her to her feet. "You better go to bed if you expect to go to work tomorrow."

At her door, he gave her a brief, nonthreatening hug. "Good night, Tory."

"Good night." Victoria entered her room, then leaned against the closed door. Today her emotions had ranged from self-pity to rage to passion. Through it all, Kane had been there. He had seen her at her worst, and continued to believe the best. The knowledge warmed her. Perhaps caring for someone wasn't so bad after all.

Sunlight filtering through gauzy white curtains woke Victoria. She glanced at her watch. 8:18. If she didn't hurry she'd be late getting to the shop for the first time in years. Throwing back the covers, she got out of bed and got dressed. The aroma of coffee greeted her the moment she reached the bottom of the stairs.

Kane glanced up when she entered the kitchen. "Good morning. Your timing is perfect. Grab a seat," he said, sliding a fluffy omelet onto her plate.

Victoria looked at the large amount of food on the table. "Do you cook for the hands as well?"

Kane sat down. "Are you saying I overdid it again?"

"I'm not saying anything." She bowed her head for Kane to say the blessing. "Amen." Picking up her fork, she cut into her cheese and ham omelet and took a small bite. Her lips closed around the food and she groaned in delight. "I might start eating breakfast every day. You're a good cook."

"I've been a bachelor for so long, I had to be." He selected a biscuit from a two-inch stack. "I gassed up your car and washed it. I hope you don't mind?"

"When did you have time?"

"This morning. I told you I'm an early riser."

Victoria was touched. "I don't mind at all. Thank you."

He nodded. "We got calls from both your grandmother and my mother this morning. They wanted to speak to you, but I told them you were asleep."

Her face heated. Slowly she put down the glass of juice she had picked up. "What did they want?"

"To get the inside track on having us to dinner first, and to see if we liked our wedding announcement in the newspapers."

"What!"

Calmly, Kane handed her two newspapers. "At least *you* look good. I can't believe Mama put my old picture in the hometown paper."

Victoria stared at their pictures. Kane looked hard. She looked sullen. "It's a tossup which one of us looks the worst," she said, then glanced up quickly at Kane to see if she had made him angry.

Kane grinned. "I think I take the honors."

"I could wring Grandmother's neck. This is all I need."

He studied her closely. "Are you worried some of your friends might have seen you yesterday at the restaurant?"

"No," she denied quickly.

Kane didn't look convinced. "Maybe I should go to the store with you."

She shook her head and stood. "No need. I'll be fine. What are you plans today?"

His narrowed gaze told her he was aware she had deliberately changed the subject. "I have a meeting at Cinnamon around ten, then I plan to do some work around the ranch."

"Then I'll see you this evening." With a forced smile, Victoria left the room.

"Kane, have you heard a word I've said?"

Slowly Kane turned from staring out the office window on the twelfth floor of the Cinnamon Corporation. A frown marched across his brow as he stared at the rotund man sitting behind a massive teak desk. "I'm sorry, William, did you say something?"

William Conrad, founder, president and CEO of *Cinnamon*, clamped his teeth tighter on his imported cigar and studied Kane over the rim of his bifocals. With a controlled motion, he sat upright in his chair. "I said, what do you think of the plans we've come up with to expand into men's skin care?"

The furrows on Kane's brow deepened.

"It's in the report I gave you." A manicured finger pointed to Kane's right hand.

Kane glanced down at the blue portfolio as if he hadn't seen it. In truth, he didn't remember taking it. Just as he didn't recall the view from the window. The landscaped grounds and surrounding office buildings hadn't existed for him. His mind was filled with visions of Victoria's determined but frightened face. She was intent on facing her problems alone.

Kane's gaze went back to William. At sixty-six, his once coal-black hair was generously sprinkled with gray and his athletic body of college days had rounded. One thing remained the same: his passion for Cinnamon. Kane didn't even think Helen, his wife of thirty odd years, came before the company. While Kane admired William's keen intelligence, he didn't agree with his priorities.

"It makes my ulcer act up just thinking of things that could go wrong with this new venture." William knocked the ash off his cigar. "Of course, I'd feel a lot better with you back here every day."

"One of us with an ulcer is enough," Kane said flatly. "I'll always appreciate being a part of the company's growth, but being a consultant on occasion is enough time spent away from my ranch."

William looked from beneath bushy brows. "You make it sound as if I welcomed you with open arms."

"You did eventually," Kane said mildly. He had expected William's resistance in taking on a partner instead of acquiring investors as he had originally planned. Kane just hadn't accepted William's decision.

"It was you or bankruptcy court, just as it was let you go gracefully two years ago or face the prospect of losing the driving force behind this company's growth," William said with a touch of irritation he didn't try to hide. "Now that you're married, you'll never come back full time. I didn't even know you were serious about anyone."

"Sometimes these things happen quickly," Kane explained. It was just his and Victoria's luck for her picture to be in the same section of the newspaper where they were running the second excerpt from a tell-all book about the rich and famous in Dallas/Fort Worth.

"As I told you earlier, she's beautiful. I probably wouldn't want to leave a woman like that either," William confessed.

"I'm not sure Helen would take that as a compliment," Kane said.

"I'm not either, so let's not tell her."

"I wouldn't think of it," Kane said, and placed the folder back on the desk, then headed for the door.

William rose out of his seat. "Where are you going? We've got to—"

"I'm well aware we have to finalize a decision in a couple of weeks if we're to hit the stores in December." Kane never slowed down. "I have something to do that can't wait."

The door closed and William slumped in his chair. "One day I'm going to have the last word with Kane."

Lavender and Lace was a madhouse. People were waiting for her when she arrived, and more came as the day wore on. Customers came into the store she hadn't seen in years. They wanted to hear all about the courtship. They ogled her ring and cast veiled glances at her stomach. The hot-pink jersey minidress she wore afforded them a good look. If it wasn't for her real friends who came by as well, she would have closed the store.

She wasn't naive enough to believe everyone had dropped by to wish her luck because she had gotten married. From the way Stephen's name kept popping into their conversation, she wondered if a few of them had heard about her altercation with him. Yet none of them were bold enough to ask outright. She had never seen so many watchful eyes and twitching ears on the alert for any hint of juicy gossip.

By 11:15 A.M. she had a raging headache. When her grandmother's lawyer stopped by, she was glad to escape. Immediately, she ushered him into her office. He stared at the marriage license she handed him so long she began to think he believed it was a forgery.

Finally, he lifted his gray head and acknowledged she'd beaten the deadline, but her grandmother could still call in the total amount of the loan if the marriage ended in less than a year. Feeling the pounding in her head increase, she walked to the front with him and said her goodbyes.

The door had barely closed behind the lawyer before it opened again. Kane's powerful body filled the doorway. Dressed in form-fitting jeans and a crisp white shirt, his appearance reminded her of their first meeting. His sweeping gaze locked on Victoria. He started toward her with a slow and purposeful gait.

A hush fell over the store. Customers parted. Kane didn't seem to notice or care. His intense gaze never left Victoria. He stopped in front of her. For a timeless moment midnight black eyes probed hers as if searching for something.

"Hi. Didn't you have a meeting?" she asked.

"Seeing you was more important."

Warmth curled though her. She realized he had been worried about her. Without thought, she placed her hand on his chest, and from somewhere, found a smile. "I'm fine."

"In that case, I'll get to the second reason I'm here." His head lowered until he heard the collective indrawn breath of several women. Grabbing Victoria's hand, he took her into her office and closed the door. Without a word, he drew her into his arms.

Her heart pounding, her eyes wide, she pressed both hands against his chest. "Th-there's no need to go any further."

"Yes, there is." His thumb grazed her lower lip. She shivered. "A woman who's been thoroughly kissed has a certain look about her. You don't have that look, but you will before you leave this room. When you go back outside there'll be no doubt why we married or why I'd fight through hell to taste your lips."

His last words ringing in her ear, his mouth closed over hers. This time she didn't think of resisting. She simply enjoyed being held and cherished. He always knew exactly what she needed.

Too soon Kane's lips and body were gone. Slowly she opened her eyes. He looked no happier than she felt. "Come on."

He didn't stop until he reached the front door. "I'll expect you at six." He opened the door and left.

Victoria touched her lips as she watched Kane get into his truck and drive away. Absently she heard the excited chatter of the women around her and knew Kane had accomplished what he had set out to do. Her reputation and her honor were intact. His timing had been perfect. Once again her knight had rescued her, but in doing so he also presented her with an even greater danger. Himself.

Returning to her office, she dialed Bonnie's art gallery. Victoria desperately needed a calming presence. She was worried about her boutiques. She was worried about being vulnerable to a man who made her blood sing. She was also sinking in quicksand and had no idea how to pull herself out. There was something to be said about living behind the safety of a castle wall.

A short time later, Victoria hung up the phone. Bonnie hadn't returned from her buying trip to New York. Victoria didn't doubt for a moment that someone in the Taggart family had called Bonnie. What concerned Victoria was that the one person she expected to receive a call from, hadn't phoned. Maybe Bonnie hadn't gotten over her fear of cupid getting an arrow in the back. All Victoria had to say was that it would be better than one in the heart.

Victoria pulled up in front of Kane's ranch house at six thirty. She meant to be home at six, but she had gotten tied up in traffic. It wouldn't hurt this one time to give in to Kane. Especially after his help that morning. But he really was going to have to learn to ask and not tell her what to do. Her pace quickened as she crossed the porch and opened the front door.

"It's about time you got home. I'm starved."

"Bonnie," Victoria shouted and ran to embrace her best friend. "I tried to call you all afternoon."

Grinning broadly, Bonnie pulled away and glanced at her husband sitting across from Kane. "Blame Dan. Kane wanted to surprise you."

"Guilty." Dan's deep mahogany face creased into a smile. Chocolate eyes sparkled devilishly. Broad shoulders and six feet of conditioned muscles, Dan was easy to talk to and fun to be with. He was the perfect husband for the light-hearted Bonnie. "I warned Kane that when you two get together, no secret is safe. I must say I never thought she'd stand not calling you all day."

"I told you, Kane asked me not to," Bonnie defended.

"I don't suppose it occurred to you to call me anyway?" Victoria asked mildly.

"It occurred to me, but I think you once compared my cousin to a bulldozer. Try bulldozer with an attitude if he doesn't get his way," Bonnie said.

"Tell me about it." Victoria smiled and looked at Kane. "It's a nice surprise. Sorry I'm late."

"Late? You're exactly on time," Bonnie said.

Victoria glanced from Bonnie to Kane. "Traffic held me up. You almost slipped up this time."

Standing, he walked to her. "A man needs a woman who'll keep him on his toes. If you want to change out of those heels, you better hurry. We don't want to make a bad impression on our guests."

"I won't be a minute." She started for the stairs, then stopped. "Where are we going?"

"Some place to have fun," Kane promised.

He was right. From the moment they entered the sports restaurant, and threw darts to select their table, to playing bingo until their orders arrived, to bowling afterwards, the evening was fun. Until Kane decided to challenge Dan to a game of pool.

"The loser has to pay the bill," Kane announced, his arm curved around Victoria's waist.

Dan rubbed his hands together. "Rack 'em up, then get out your wallet."

"You and Bonnie don't have a chance against a team like us."

"Us?" Victoria echoed. "I don't know how to play pool."

Kane shrugged broad shoulders. "It's easy. I'll teach you, Honey."

Learning the "Cotton-Eyed Joe" had been child's play when compared to the coordination and eye control needed to shoot the cue ball from where it lay and strike the object ball into one of the six pockets. Victoria never accomplished one shot correctly. She couldn't concentrate. Kane had *insisted* on "helping her" when it was her turn.

Every time she bent over the table with her cue stick, her hips brushed intimately against Kane, who stood behind coaching her. Her insides tingled. She had the strangest urge to rub her hips against the bluntness she felt. Half ashamed and half aroused, she missed shot after shot. The game ended in total defeat for the Taggarts.

She handed Kane her cue. "Sorry. At least Bonnie managed to pocket one ball."

"Winning isn't always important. It's how you play the game," he told her, his voice deep and husky.

Victoria didn't say anything, she couldn't. Her body's sudden need overrode everything else. The same need was mirrored in Kane's beautiful eyes. She felt hot, restless and up to her waist in quicksand. She wanted him. Badly. She didn't know what frightened her more, her emotional vulnerability or her fear that if she gave in to her desire, Kane would find her lacking as a woman.

Arriving home, she started for the safety of her room. Kane's deep voice called after her. "How about a game of dominoes?"

She spoke without turning. "I've lost enough for one night." Spending more time with Kane was asking for trouble.

Kane's velvet laughter followed her up the stairs. "Good night, Honey."

After breakfast the next morning, Kane waved goodbye without asking what time she planned to be home. Victoria made it a point to be home by six. For once she was going to win the mind game.

Seeing no food on the stove, she smiled. Until she opened the refrigerator and saw two large T-bone steaks marinating and a mixed salad. She was leaving the kitchen to change clothes when the back door opened.

"Hi, Honey," Kane said, his hand still on the doorknob. Perspiration beaded his brow and soaked the front of his plaid shirt. "One of the horses pulled a tendon and I'm in the barn with the vet. If you're hungry, everything is ready."

"How bad is it?" she asked.

Kane's brow lifted as if he hadn't expected her to ask. "Doc Hamil doesn't think the problem is serious."

She nodded, feeling at odds. "You better get back. I'll wait for you. Do you want a baked potato?"

His smile lit his dark brown face and lifted his mustache. "They're in the warming oven."

"Oh."

"I better go. I'll be back as soon as I can." He turned, then paused. "Thanks for being willing to wait. I enjoy my meals better with you."

Victoria stared at the closed door a long time. Didn't Kane have any walls, any defenses? He wasn't the least bit bothered by letting her see he was genuinely happy to see her. Then, she remembered their talk in the meadow. She wondered when his patience would run out and he'd get tired of her, and of cooking all the meals.

After two weeks of marriage, Kane continued to have meals ready when Victoria arrived home. Sometimes he treated her more like a guest than a wife. Other times, he let her know he expected her to be an equal partner in the marriage even if she wasn't sure about anything else.

"I am not getting on that animal."

"Tory, the only way to really see the ranch is on horseback," Kane explained.

Arms held stiffly by her side, Victoria stared at the sleek black horse being held by Kane. "I'm sorry, but horses and I don't get along very well. One threw me in summer camp when I was in the sixth grade. I made a promise then that if they'd keep away from me, I'd keep away from them."

"The counselor didn't put you back on?"

"He tried." The lift of her chin spoke volumes.

Another case of not trusting, Kane thought. Tory wasn't much on giving anyone, man or beast, another chance. Yet he had to teach her to try. She had to learn she could trust him with her emotions as well as with her body.

Kane glanced around and saw Pete heading for

the barn. He was the oldest of Kane's hired hands and the hardest working. The retired bullfighter wasn't happy unless he was busy.

"Pete, take Mirage back and unsaddle her, then come back and get Shadow Walker's saddle."

"Sure thing, boss." Pete's gloved hand closed over the reins. Passing Victoria, he tipped his battered straw hat. "Evenin', Mrs. Taggart."

"Hello, Pete," she said absently, her gaze on her husband instead of the wiry ranch hand.

Kane unsaddled his quarterhorse, then tossed the saddle on the top rung of the coral.

"You aren't angry, are you?"

He sent her a look over his shoulder. "I told you that you can say 'no' to me anytime." Catching the horse's mane, he swung onto its back. "Some things I'll accept. Your fear of horses isn't one of them. Come here."

Victoria took a step backward. Riding bareback with Kane would be more terrifying than riding by herself. Lately, when he smiled at her, she had the craziest urge to touch him. She looked toward the security of the house, a hundred yards away.

"I don't know if I mentioned it, but I've been riding since I was three years old. I'd catch you before you got ten feet."

Her chin went up again. "I'm not some animal."

"No, you're my wife. All I'm asking is that you

come over here and close your eyes. Think of something nice and before you know it, you'll be up here with me. If you're still uneasy, I'll put you down." He held out his hand.

She shook her head, sending her ponytail swinging. "I just finished dinner."

"If cowboys waited for the meals to settle before they got on a horse, the West would still need settling," Kane told her.

"They were used to it. I'm not." She took a step backward, then another.

"Then you're going to give up, and let me be embarrassed in two weeks?" he asked mildly.

She stopped. "What are you talking about?"

"Every year I have a group of kids from the Forth Worth Youth Center over for an old-fashioned hayride and barbecue. I wanted you riding beside me."

She knew she was being set up. The trouble was, she didn't see how to get out of it. Yet. "I'll ride with the driver of the hay wagon."

"Counselors already have dibs on those seats. Of course you could ride in the back with the kids. I'll get you some ear plugs to protect your ears from their loud radios."

"Kane, don't think for a minute I don't know you're doing a number on me."

He grinned. "Guilty, but I'm also telling you the

truth." The grin dissolved. "Last year Pete was sick and I drove the wagon. I wanted them to have a good time, so I didn't complain about the noise. The counselor said the kids say music sounds better if it's loud. It must have sounded fantastic."

Her resistance faded. So she wasn't the only one Kane gave to. He was genuinely kind. "If I fall off that horse and get killed, I'm going to come back and haunt you." Taking a deep breath, she walked to his horse and closed her eyes.

Warm hands closed around her waist. She concentrated on them. "You all right?"

Her eyes opened. She sat sideways on the horse. Kane's arm circled her waist and brushed the underside of her breasts. Careful not to look down, she nodded.

"Slide your leg over to the other side and lean back against me."

Swallowing, she slowly complied. Heat and conditioned muscles pressed against her back, and on either side of her legs. This was worse than she imagined. She tried to swallow again and couldn't. Her throat was too dry.

"We're only going a little ways. Since you don't have a saddle to keep you on the horse I'm going to keep one arm around your waist so you won't slide off. All you have to do is lean against me. I'd put you behind me, but I don't want you letting go and falling or shutting your eyes so tight you don't see a thing."

The horse took off at a slow walk. Victoria clutched the muscled arm circling her waist. She felt off-balance by the rocking motion as much as by Kane's closeness. "Kane?"

"I got you, honey. I'll have you riding in no time, but then again, this is more enjoyable." His warm breath caressed her ear. "Just relax, try to feel the motion of the horse and think of something pleasant."

All she could think of was Kane. She never imagined horseback riding as being sensual before, but her mind was conjuring up all sorts of things. None of them conducive to remaining impartial and upright. She was relieved when he stopped by the bank of a small stream.

Getting off, he pulled her into his arms and started walking toward a crop of trees. "Won't your horse run off?"

"Shadow Walker is too well mannered for that."

Victoria had a feeling that if anything or anyone was foolish enough to run away from Kane he'd come after them. "It may come as a shock to you, but I've been walking since I was nine months old."

"I like carrying you. Besides your fancy outfit would be ruined." He gave her oversized white blouse and black gabardine slacks a sweeping glance. "I thought we discussed you getting some other clothes."

Feeling more at ease, she smiled into his frowning face. "We did, in passing. The only things sturdier I have are a fantastic denim skirt and shirt trimmed in turquoise leather with a matching pair of custom-made boots. I wore them to a dance to celebrate the contributions of black men in settling the West."

"The 'forgotten cowboys'," Kane said. "One in every five cowboys was black."

"Exactly. I didn't know until that night that a black man named Estavanico helped discover Texas." She tried to look up in Kane's face. "I would think you would have been there. Cleo Hearn of Lancaster and a lot of other cowboys like Donald and Ronald Stephens from Oklahoma were there." She frowned. "Despite their last name, they were very nice. I met my first authentic cowgirl, Marilyn LaBlanc. I'm surprised you weren't there."

"I'm not much on social functions." Kane stopped beneath a willow tree on the sloping bank of a stream and sat down with her in his arms. "We'll go into town tomorrow and get you some jeans and proper boots."

She jerked upright in his lap. "My outfit will do for the youth outing."

"Not if you want to blend in. Besides, I told

you I like riding everyday, and I'd like you to go with me. I don't mind riding double, if you don't."

She looked into his stern face. "I'll pick up something after work tomorrow."

"Jeans, but I'd like to go with you to get the boots. Buy the wrong pair and your feet will pay the price forever."

She started to tell him she was capable of buying a pair of boots, then changed her mind. Kane had a stubborn streak sometimes, and she knew he wasn't above putting her in the truck and taking her despite her protests. The trouble was, his stubbornness was usually for her benefit.

How do you fight a gentle, protective man who has your best interest at heart? "All right. I think I'll walk back."

"Not in those play shoes." Gathering her closer, he rose in one lithe movement. "Once we're home you can walk around until you wear a trench in the yard."

"Anyone ever tell you how bossy you are?"

"Once or twice."

Chapter 11

The next day when Victoria came home from work, Kane was waiting for her. Black Stetson pushed back on his head, one booted foot crossed over the other at the ankle, he leaned against the porch post with folded arms. "You ready to go shopping?" he asked as soon as Victoria's sandaled foot touched the bottom wooden step.

"I suppose if I refused, your reply will be 'walking or over your shoulder'," she tossed, feeling unexpectantly jubilant at the thought of verbal sparing with him.

"Actually I was thinking of something else," he drawled.

"Such as?"

Unfolding his arms and body in one fluid movement, he walked to the edge of the porch. "This."

Strong hands lifted her; gentle lips closed over hers. The kiss was slow and drugging. After a long moment his head lifted. "Do we go shopping for your boots or keep on kissing?"

Heavy lidded eyes opened. Victoria realized her feet were on the step again, but their bodies still touched. She looked at Kane's lips, felt the erratic beat of his heart, knew hers wasn't any steadier. For the first time the knowledge didn't frighten her. From Kane she had known only tenderness, the same tenderness with which he now held her.

"What's the third choice?" she asked breathlessly.

He blinked, then threw back his dark head. Velvet laughter rumbled from his throat. "Tory, you finally got one over on me." Curving his arm around her waist he started for his truck, parked in front of her Jaguar.

"I told you I would." Smiling, she started to get into the truck, then stopped. "You opened the wrong door."

"No I didn't. If you're going to be the wife of a cowboy you might as well learn how to properly ride in a truck." He urged her inside on the driver's side. "Couples sit so close you can't tell where the man stops and his woman begins."

Victoria inched across the seat. "Kane, I'm not so sure we should carry things this far."

"I am. In fact I've been thinking about it all day." He slid in beside her. "You aren't afraid are you?"

"What do you think?" she answered evasively.

"I think you're the most beautiful woman in the world and I'm proud to call you my wife," Kane told her softly, his knuckles grazed across her jaw.

Her heart skipped a beat. "You're not so bad yourself," she said just as softly.

Kane started the engine and pulled off. "After we get your boots, we better have your eyes tested."

"My judgment is faulty at times, but my vision is twenty/twenty." Tentatively, she touched his hand, trying to give him the reassurance he had given her so many times. "In the ways that count you have no equal. No matter what happens, remember that."

"I'll always remember everything about you." He turned onto the Farm and Market Road. "I think you might look good in red boots."

Victoria willingly let Kane change the subject. "Only if you get a matching pair."

"You're getting too good at this."

"Ain't I though?"

"Mrs. Taggart, thank you again for letting the kids come out so soon after your marriage. We are all so thrilled for you and Kane. You two looked good riding side by side."

Victoria smiled at the elderly black woman. "Mrs. Sanders, please call me Victoria. I'll let you in on a little secret. Kane only recently started giving me riding lessons."

The gray-headed woman stopped dishing out potato salad. "No wonder Kane offered to let you ride on his horse with him."

Victoria blushed. "Kane likes to tease."

"He looks happier than I've ever seen him and we've been friends for five years," the other woman said.

"Mrs. Sanders, am I going to get any potato salad or not?" asked an ebony-hued teenager.

She glanced at the young man, an ear stud in his left ear and three inches of hair sticking up from the crown of his otherwise closely shaven head. "Keep on with that attitude and you might not."

The boy behind the impatient youth snickered. Mrs. Sanders shot him a look. "That goes for you too, Emmanuel."

Both boys cut their eyes at Victoria and tucked their heads. "However, since it was my fault for not paying attention, I apologize. Can't have the two star players of the baseball team hungry." She dumped an extra portion on both plates.

The young men straightened, their pride intact, and moved down the line to where several other volunteers handed out beef brisket, corn on the cob, and soft drinks.

"You handled them well," Victoria commented.

"I didn't always. You should see Kane with them. He's a natural father."

Victoria's hand paused in serving baked beans on the plate of the last person in line. "Yes . . . he's very caring."

"Forgive me for saying so, but you're not what we expected." Steadily working, Mrs. Sanders kept talking. "We all saw your picture in the paper with the announcement, and you looked a little tight in the shoes."

Victoria recalled having the picture taken for her thirtieth birthday. She had looked straight at the camera as if daring it to do its worst. It had. "I didn't want my picture made, but my grandmother insisted. I'm afraid it showed."

"I liked it."

Victoria glanced up to see Kane grinning at her. He did that a lot lately and more and more she found herself grinning back, as she was doing now. "You're just asking to wear these beans."

"On my plate is fine," he said, waiting until she complied, then he moved down the food line.

Shortly, he returned holding a cardboard bottom of the soft drink case he had converted into a tray. Inside was a plate laden with food. "I've already staked us out a quiet spot."

Trying to ignore Mrs. Sanders's indulgent smile, Victoria followed Kane to a blanket under one of the many oak trees in the back yard. In the middle of the blanket was a card that read 'reserved.'

"Quite inventive." Victoria sat down and crossed her jean-clad legs over her new black eel-skin boots.

"I thought so. Here, hold this and I'll go get us a couple of drinks."

Leaning against the tree, Victoria watched Kane cross the yard. The graceful power of his muscular body drew her eyes like a magnet. He had only gone a few feet when he was stopped by one of the youths, then another youngster joined them. A couple of times, he glanced back as he moved slowly toward the ice cooler. She waved her hand in understanding.

The teenagers, between thirteen and sixteen, vied for Kane's time and his attention. She couldn't blame them. She had sought solace in his arms and had never been disappointed. Kane gave without making you feel less for needing to ask.

She wasn't surprised when five of the twenty kids came back with him. He looked apologetic, then pained as another youngster dropped down on the blanket, music blaring from his boom box. Kane glanced at Victoria.

She shrugged her shoulders. "When in Rome."

"I brought my algebra grade up and I'm going to pass," boasted a pimply faced boy, his baseball cap on backward, his teeth bared in a wide grin.

Kane slapped him on his broad shoulders. "I told you. Some of us have to study harder than others."

"What did you ever have to do that was hard?" snarled a voice that plainly couldn't decide what pitch to maintain. "You have everything. A nice place. A rich, pretty wife."

Kane lifted a brow at the thin young man standing belligerently over him. "I worked on my father's farm two hours before school and until dark after I got home. I didn't expect people to give me anything. The world doesn't owe you anything, Ali, and thinking that it does is going to leave you bitter and angry."

"I've got a right . . ."

"Says who? You're barely sixteen. If you want to reach seventeen happy, change your attitude and try to figure out how the system works instead of working against it."

"That's selling out."

"That's surviving. Then you can help someone else have a better life."

Ali dug the toe of his well-worn sneaker into the lush grass. "I'll think about it," he said sullenly.

"You do that. In the meantime, stop standing over my wife and have a seat." Kane said. "And if you keep on trying to ruin the day for everyone, I might put Mrs. Taggart on your softball team as a pitcher."

The young man looked horrified. Victoria glared at Kane. "Did I ever tell you that the year I was the pitcher on the girls' softball team in high school we went to state?"

Kane's mouth dropped open.

"I know it's hard to close your mouth with your foot inside, but try," Victoria said sweetly.

The kids looked from Kane to Victoria, then they all burst into laughter.

Kane took the converted tray out of her hands and pulled her into his arms before she could protest. She could only accept and enjoy the brief kiss he gave her.

The boys whistled. The girls giggled.

He lifted his head. "I've got a feeling I'm going to pay for that remark for a long time." Sitting her upright, he picked up their food. "You know I was kidding, Tory. We're a team. We're going to beat all comers in every event."

"Event?"

"Three-legged race, sack race, water balloon

toss." He eyed her cotton blouse. "Maybe we won't enter the balloon toss."

Victoria smiled. "Yes, we will. I am going to show you exactly how good I can throw."

Victoria and Kane lost every event.

In the three-legged race she fell on top of him within five feet of the finish line. They lay grinning from ear to ear at each other. Two hops and she was out of the sack race. Kane landed beside her. The softball game was a tie between the adults and the youths. Victoria pitched to Kane's loud praise and encouragement.

When it came time for the water balloon throw, the counselor couldn't find the balloons. From the hunches and grins the boys were giving each other, Victoria deduced they had helped a little with their disappearance. One of the girls suggested a dance. The boom box blared out.

"Wanna dance?"

Leaning back on the blanket, Victoria glanced at Kane beside her. "I don't think my feet can move that fast."

"They don't have to." Pulling her up and into his arms, he held her close. "Listen to the music inside your head."

Her head pressed against his chest, she followed his lead. As warmth and need coursed through her, everything else ceased to exist. She felt cherished, needed, wanted.

The intrusive noise of whistles and applause caused her to lift her head. All the other couples had stopped dancing and moved back to watch Kane and Victoria. A few of the women counselors were dabbing their eyes, the men were giving Kane a thumb's up sign, the young girls looked dreamy, the boys surprised but pleased.

"It's nice to know love still exists," Mrs. Sanders said. "We've taken up enough of your time. You've only been married a month. Come on, people, and let's get the place cleaned up."

With a light squeeze and a brush of his lips, Kane went to help. Her mind in a turmoil, Victoria didn't move. She had forgotten about her boutiques and their business agreement. Frantically, she thought back and realized she had stopped thinking about the reason for their marriage after Kane kissed her earlier on the blanket. She had been a woman enjoying the day with a man she cared about.

"Tory, are you all right?"

She glanced up into Kane's ruggedly masculine face. If she didn't watch herself, when the time came, she wouldn't be able to walk away. "I'm just tired."

"Go on inside and rest. I'll explain to everyone."

"No, I'll be all right. You go on." She watched Kane help load up the van and knew she lied. She would never be all right if she didn't stay away from him.

Something was wrong. Kane knew it, but he wasn't sure what to do about it. He looked across the breakfast table at Victoria's bowed head. The only reason she sat there was because this morning she had been unable to think of an excuse fast enough. This was the first meal they had shared in a week. Where he was, Victoria wasn't.

It was usually dark when she arrived home. Mumbling that she had work to do, she closed herself in her room. He didn't know what had changed at the outing, but maybe tonight after the banquet they'd have a chance to talk.

"I'll pick you up around four."

Her head jerked up. "For what?"

"The banquet in Houston honoring black men who have made a significant difference in the community. A friend of mine is flying us down," he explained patiently. "I told you Monday."

Victoria put her fork beside the uneaten stack of pancakes. "I was out of the shop last Saturday. I can't be gone again."

"You can if you want to." Some of Kane's

patience slipped. Maybe it was time to push again. "I made room reservations so you can rest and get dressed in Houston. After the banquet, we can stay over and fly back tomorrow."

"No." She stood. "I have to stay and work. You go and have a good trip."

"It's important to me that you go."

She stopped, but didn't turn. "I have things to do. Perhaps it's best if we don't become too involved in each other's lives. Remember, our marriage is only a business agreement."

Kane's large hands fisted on the table. "I thought we were . . . never mind. I'll see you tonight."

She glanced over her shoulder. "Since you'll be late coming back, I think I'll stay at my place."

Something hard flashed across Kane's face. "*This* is *your place* and you had better be *here* when I get home or I'm coming to get you."

"I'm tired of you bossing me. I can't wait until my time is up so I can get back to living my own life," she snapped, then ran to her car.

Tears rolled down her cheek and splattered on her blouse as she drove out of the yard. She didn't notice or care. She remembered the pain in Kane's face. She fought against going back and telling him she was sorry. For her own protection, she couldn't.

If things continued, she'd end up in Kane's bed.

Once that happened she would be more vulnerable than she had ever been in her life. She couldn't put herself in that position again for anyone.

Victoria had the worst morning of her life. Realizing she wasn't going to be any good on the sales floor, she called in a part-time sales clerk and went to her office. However, she couldn't concentrate enough to work on the books, the time schedule, her summer sale promotion plans or any of the dozen things that needed her attention.

Each time the phone rang, she'd look at it and wonder if it was Kane. Then when her intercom didn't light up, disappointment would wash over her and she'd wonder how he was doing.

As the clock moved toward three, her restlessness grew. She wouldn't put it past Kane to make her go. Then she remembered the look on his face and knew he wouldn't come for her. Whatever feelings he might have had for her, she had effectively killed them. That had been her intention, but she hadn't counted on the pain for either of them.

It was after one in the morning when she pulled up in front of the ranch house. A single light burned in the kitchen. She didn't know if Kane had tried to make good his promise to come get her or not.

Ten minutes after three, she had left the shop

and gone to an eight-screen theater. She hadn't been able to sit through more than three movies before the theater closed. Getting out of the car, she didn't know whether she was happy or disappointed not to see Kane's truck in the driveway.

Unlocking the front door, she reached for the light switch.

"So you finally decided to come home."

Fear splinted through her at the rough, unfamiliar voice. She fumbled for the switch. Light flared. Frantically, her gaze searched the room until she located Matt standing at the foot of the stairs. A part of her wanted to relax, but something about his eyes wouldn't let her. "Where's Kane?"

He didn't say anything, just continued to stare at her. "Answer me. Where's Kane? Has something happened to him?"

"Would you care?" he asked, his voice as hard as his face.

Fear congealed in the pit of her stomach. She ran toward the stairs. "I'll find him myself."

"He's not there." His words stopped her midway across the room.

"Where is he?"

"He went looking for you. For the life of me I can't understand why, after what you put him through tonight."

"What are you talking about?"

He snorted. "Don't try to act innocent. Kane knew he had a good chance of receiving the Man of the Year Award tonight. He asked you to go with him, didn't he?"

Victoria felt ill. "He asked, but . . . I didn't know he was up for an award."

"He won. His family was there, but not his beautiful bride. She was too busy with her stores to bother coming. Every man sitting on the platform had a woman with him except Kane. He refused to let Mama or Addie take your place. You can imagine some of the things people said."

Victoria closed her eyes, her heart going out to Kane. She had hurt him, trying to protect herself.

"What's your price?"

Her eyelids flicked upward. "Price?"

Matt's smile left her chilled. "I'm going to save Kane from the hard lesson I learned about beautiful women and lying eyes. One Taggart strolling in hell is enough." He took a step closer. "A blind man can see Kane cares about you, but only a blind man would believe you cared about him in return. Name your price and walk away. I'll give you whatever you want if you'll go upstairs and pack your bags before he returns."

"If you weren't Kane's brother, I'd ask you to leave. I'll wait for Kane upstairs." She started past him.

"In your own solitary bed no doubt."

Surprise stopped her as effectively as if she had run into a glass wall. Words of denial formed in her mind until she saw the derision in Matt's eyes, heard it in his voice.

"I just discovered why Kane was so insistent that I not return with him. There's only one guest bedroom and you're sleeping in it. The others are full of unfinished antiques. He's too good to get kicked in the teeth like this."

"I wouldn't hurt him." Even as Victoria spoke the words, she knew that was exactly what she had done over and over.

"You don't think sleeping in the guest bedroom would hurt him? What kind of wife are you? You wouldn't even give him that little of yourself."

She flinched.

Unrelenting fingers grabbed her arm. "Name your price."

"Let her go, Matt." Kane ordered.

Chapter 12

Matt neither moved nor did he take his cutting gaze from Victoria's uplifted face. "I hope no one uses you the way you're using Kane."

Without thought Stephen came to Victoria's mind. Bile rose in her throat. My God! Had she treated Kane the same deplorable way Stephen did her? The realization that she had, struck her with the force of a physical blow. By trying to protect herself she had hurt Kane with the same selfish ruthlessness Stephen dealt her.

Matt's fingers slowly unclamped. Stepping back, he faced his brother. "I'll sleep in the bunk house."

Kane kept his gaze on Victoria until he heard the front door open and close.

"Please forgive me. I didn't know," Victoria cried, anguish in her voice.

"Like you said, we have to get used to each other not being around." He walked past her and up the stairs.

Not knowing what to say, Victoria went to her room. Restless, she paced the floor. She knew from experience the pain Kane must be suffering. Even when she no longer cared about Stephen, the idea that he thought she wasn't woman enough, intelligent enough, beautiful enough, hurt. A caring man like Kane didn't deserve to be hurt because she was a coward.

Trembling fingers opened the door connecting their bedrooms. What she saw made her heart constrict. Kane, his elbows bent, his bowed head resting wearily in the open palms of his hands, sat in an overstuffed chair in the far corner of the room. "Kane."

Abruptly his head lifted. For a moment he looked like a wild animal trapped in his lair, then his expression became guarded. "What are you doing in here?"

Knowing she was to blame for the bleakness in his once-tender voice, she took a tentative step toward him. "Trying to apologize *again*."

"If you don't mind, I'm tired." Pushing to his feet, he pulled the dangling black bow tie from around his neck and flung it toward the bed. It missed. So did the black tuxedo jacket that followed.

For once he didn't appear concerned with neatness. Victoria was all too aware of the reason why. "Matt told me you won the Man of the Year Award. You must be very proud." She glanced around the room she had always been afraid to enter. She wasn't surprised by the antique mahogany furniture, but she was by the massive sleigh bed. Then she remembered the yearning she heard sometimes in his voice, saw in his face. Kane was a romantic. He still dreamed, and she had taken one of his dreams. "Where is your award?"

"In the car." His shirt landed in the vicinity of the other discarded clothes. Unbuckling his belt, he stared at her. "Do you mind?"

Victoria looked into his drawn face and felt his misery and need as if it came from her own body. Kane needed her just as she needed him. "Of course not." Pushing his hands aside, she pulled the belt from the loops.

"What are you doing?" Kane yelled as he staggered back.

"Helping you," she said, hoping she sounded braver than her shaking knees indicated. "I know I haven't been very good at it before, but I had you confused with someone else. I don't any more."

"That's not what you're doing," Kane told her. "I heard what Matt told you and I don't need your pity."

"I'm not giving you any," Victoria answered softly.

Kane was not convinced. "Then what do you call your sudden need to come in here?"

"I hurt you and—"

"I thought so," Kane interrupted, his eyes blazing. "I can do without you offering your body on the sacrificial altar just because you're feeling guilty."

Incensed, Victoria gave him glare for glare. "How dare you say I'd go to bed with you out of guilt."

"It's the truth. Nothing else has prompted you to approach me first." Kane shouted back. "I can count on one hand the number of times you've willingly touched me. Now you think I'm fool enough to believe you can't wait to crawl in bed with me? Well, I'm not that hard up or that stupid."

Grabbing her arm, he started for the connecting bedroom door. "I'm doing us both a favor. In the morning you'd feel sorry you ever let me touch you and run like hell."

"Not if you did it right," she blurted out.

Kane went deathly still.

Knowing she finally had his attention, she looked at his hard face and rushed on. "I know I haven't had much experience in these matters, but it seems reasonable that *if* a man can make a woman scream in pleasure, she wouldn't be sorry afterwards or in a hurry to leave."

Kane's fingers tightened on her arm, but he made no other move one way or the other. Victoria decided to push him a little. "Or was it just a cowboy bragging?"

His eyes drilled into her. Victoria lowered her gaze to the middle of his wide naked chest. "I might have known. In all the risqué discussions I've heard at the beauty salon about a man's prowess in bed, I've never heard of a man making a woman scream." She sighed dramatically. "You probably can crimp a lot of toes though. Ethel, my beautician, says if her toes don't crimp, she feels cheated."

Victoria glanced up at Kane's scowling face. "Oh, well, it was an interesting thought."

Powerful hands clasped her arms and jerked her to him. Nose to nose, eye to eye, he snarled, actually snarled, at her. She had the feeling that Kane fought the urge to shake her. With her feet dangling in the air, he started for his bed.

"So you think I was bragging. So you think you might like to scream. Well, Victoria Elizabeth

Chandler Taggart, you pushed this cowboy too hard this time." He tossed her on the bed.

Victoria bounced up, her arms flailing out to maintain her balance. Once equilibrium was achieved, she brushed her hair out of her eyes and wished she hadn't. Hands on hips, feet spread apart, Kane looked dangerous, yet he didn't move from his threatening position. Then she remembered that this was Kane. He would hurt himself before he harmed her. He wanted her to run.

"If your intention is to make me scream by glaring at me, it won't work. As much as I enjoy looking at your magnificent body, I'd much rather have it next to mine."

"You're asking for it, Tory."

She tilted her head. "Am I going to get it?" she asked, her voice husky. "I want to be able to touch you without debating the wisdom of doing so. I've been running from you all week because I knew if I didn't, I'd run *to* you. I had stopped thinking of you as my business partner and started thinking of you as a man I cared about, a man I wanted to be intimate with." She took a deep breath.

"Despite everything I know about you and our agreement that I be there for you, I ran. I disregarded your feelings in an attempt to protect mine."

"Tory, don't—"

"Even now, you're trying to spare me. Not this

time. I was wrong. It was utterly selfish of me to run out on you yesterday. I . . . I know that nothing I can say or do will erase the pain I caused, but I am sorry. The odd thing is, running only made me more miserable."

Hope and tears gleamed in her eyes. "I want to stop being afraid of my emotions. No other man can give me that freedom except you. I know I'm asking a lot after the way I behaved, but . . . but I thought since I was giving this time too, and I'm a little scared how this is going to turn out, it might count for something."

For a long time, Kane simply stared at her, then his hands moved to his side. "It counts for a lot."

"Oh, Kane." Victoria scrambled to her knees and into his arms. His lips took hers in a kiss filled with passion and long-suppressed hunger. She trembled, loving the feel of his warm muscled flesh beneath her seeking fingers. Their mouths clung as if both were starved and were finally feasting at a banquet.

"Please be sure. There isn't anything I wouldn't give to be buried so deep inside you that there would be no beginning and no end. To hear your cries of passion and know I pulled them from your lips." His hands trembled. "I'm not sure if I can stop once we start or if I could survive if you turned away from me."

Shaking fingers smoothed the frown from his brow. "I'm sure. The lack is mine, not yours." Her gaze fell. "I-I'm not very good at this."

Kane snorted. Hard fingers lifted her chin and pulled her closer. His hips moved. Victoria gasped as she felt the frank hardness of his desire. "If you were any better, I don't think I could stand it. Last chance to run for the door.'

She kissed him, giving him everything, holding back nothing of the hunger she felt. She was tired of being afraid. Need shimmered through her. She leaned back and Kane followed her down into the waiting softness of the mattress. His body against hers felt glorious, but she wanted to know how it would feel if there was nothing between them.

Her breath caught when he started to unbutton her blouse. He released the front fasteners of her lacy blue bra. Air rushed over her lips in a ragged sigh. His callused hand cupped her aching breast. She wanted to moan with pleasure and scream with impatience at the same time. "Kane?"

"We waited so long, Tory. You feel good, too damn good," Kane growled, his mouth closing over her nipple. Then his hand swept up her skirt, over her legs, between her thighs. Instinctively, her knees clamped together. But as Kane's gentle finger stroked her inner softness, she arched against his hand in pleasure. A moan slipped past her lips.

"You were made to be loved by me," Kane half-groaned, half-growled. Quickly, he dispensed with her clothes, then tore open a foil package. Finally she was beneath him, feeling the heat and hardness of his body. Their eyes met a second before he eased into her.

Kane wanted to keep his eyes open, to watch the emotions sweep across her face, but the pleasure was too exquisite, too intense. His lids fluttered. Her long sleek legs wrapped around him, drawing him deeper inside her satin heat.

When the scream came, neither knew whose it was.

Victoria woke slowly, savoring the delicious way she felt. Opening her eyes, she saw Kane, his elbow bent, his chin propped in his open palm, staring down at her. Sunlight flowed over his broad shoulders, bronzing his skin. He looked beautiful and glowing. She had put that look on his face. She was wildly pleased.

She smiled shyly. "Good morning."

Leaning over, he brushed his lips across hers. "Now it is."

"I-I planned to be up first and serve you breakfast in bed," she said, her voice quaky as his thumb stroked her rigid nipple through the sheet.

Kane's eyes shimmered. "Exactly what I had in

mind." The sheet slid away. His mouth closed over the pouting point.

"K-Kane" Victoria's voice broke; she tried again. "I need to go to the kitchen . . . oh, goodness." His head moved across the flatness of her stomach, going steadily lower. Understanding dawned. "Kane, you—" Victoria sucked in her breath as Kane found what he sought.

Victoria's last coherent thought before pleasure overtook her was that besides making her scream, Kane was probably the best toe crimper in the world.

Much later that morning, hunger drove Victoria and Kane to the kitchen. Kane had on his jeans; Victoria wore his white shirt. Kane had personally put it on her and rolled up several inches of dangling sleeves, saying she wouldn't stay dressed long enough to bother putting on anything else.

Arms folded, Victoria leaned against the counter and shamelessly studied Kane's hips as he bent to pull out a package of giant blueberry muffins from the refrigerator. To think, she had once been afraid of showing her emotions around him. She felt freer and happier than she had in her entire life. Closing the door, he turned to see her appreciative smile.

"You have a nice set of buns, cowboy."

Kane gave her a crooked grin. Setting the muffins aside, he pulled her into his arms and nuzzled her neck. "You think so, huh?"

"Hmm," Victoria almost purred as she arched her neck. "If you don't stop doing that, the bacon will burn."

"I might consider it, provided you stop moving against me as if you have an itch only I can scratch."

"One of us has to be sensible," Victoria said, then nipped his shoulder.

His hands cupped her hips and fitted her softness against his hardness, his lips searching for hers. "I don't think it's going to be me."

The back door opened. Through the half slit of her eyes Victoria saw Matt, his jaw slack, poised in the doorway. With a shriek, she tried to hide behind Kane, who had turned toward the door.

"Morning, Matt," Kane said, his voice strained. "Can you come back in a little while?"

Matt shook his dark head. "Just wanted to let you know, Pete is driving me to DFW to catch a flight home."

Kane nodded. "Have a safe trip. I'll call you later."

"Are you sure this is what you want?" Matt asked, his probing gaze searching his brother's face before going to the tousled head of black hair that had momentarily popped from behind Kane's back.

"Yes." Kane spoke without hesitation.

He nodded in resignation. "Then I'll see you at Addie's graduation ceremonies next weekend." The door closed.

"I don't think he likes me," Victoria said. "But then I haven't given him much reason to."

Kane stroked her face with his knuckles. "He'll come around. He had a bad experience with a woman and he doesn't want me to do the same."

A look of shame crossed her face. "I never intended to hurt you, but I did."

"You were afraid to trust. You've taken a big step and we'll take one day at a time."

"Is that what you want?"

Kane brushed her hair away from her face. "No. I'm a greedy man, I want it all. But like I told you once, I'd settle for a lot less."

Victoria breathed a little easier. She wanted it all too, but she learned long ago that wanting wasn't enough. In time, maybe they would learn what was enough. "I think I'm a little greedy too."

"I aim to satisfy all of your needs." A flick of his wrist cut the burner off, then he pulled out a chair. Victoria gasped softly to find herself straddling Kane's legs. "Scared?"

With her knees on either side of his waist, she was exposed and vulnerable. Her hands clamped on his shoulders felt the heat of his flesh even as she felt the tender way his hands held her waist. "Not me. Are you?"

"I like a sassy woman." He devoured her lips. When he lifted his head, both were breathing a little harder. "I was a fool to start something I'd have to wait to finish."

"One of us is crazy." She moved against the obvious proof of his ability to finish what he had started.

He laughed wickedly. "Me." Standing with her in his arms, he left the room. "Breakfast will have to wait."

"Why are we going back upstairs?"

"Birth control. I told you I'd always take care of you, and that means no unplanned pregnancy," Kane said. "I'd be the happiest man on earth to have a child with you, but I don't think you're ready for that big of a step in our relationship."

She blushed and buried her head between his neck and shoulder. After all the things she had done with him and to him, the subject of birth control shouldn't have embarrassed her. But it did. It also reminded her of how caring Kane was of her. She just wasn't sure if this time she agreed with him.

"If they don't stop ringing the doorbell, I'm going to strangle them," Kane growled, positioning one jean-clad leg between Victoria's bare ones.

"M-Maybe it's important," she said, her voice breathless and thick.

"Nothing is more important than this." Kane's tongue swept inside her mouth. Instantly her tongue sought his. Her arms tightened around his neck. Her body yielded. Desire rocked through him.

He pressed her deeper into the mattress. Restlessly, his hand swept over the silken skin of her stomach to the soft inner flesh of her thigh. Blunt-tipped fingers lifted the edge of her panties.

The chime of the doorbell was suddenly accompanied by what sounded like a fist pounding against the door. With a muttered expletive, Kane rolled from atop Victoria and snatched his shirt from the floor.

"I have to go to work anyway," Victoria said huskily. Sitting up, she fumbled with the clasp of her lacy red bra. "Mondays are always hectic at the store."

"Don't you move from that bed," Kane ordered. Shoving his arms into the shirt, he reached for the doorknob. "For their sake, I hope they have hospitalization."

Kane recalled few times that he had been so angry. He had finally managed to get Victoria to change her mind about going to work, and now some nut was making a nuisance of himself. During their lovemaking, she held nothing back and came to him with a passion and need that equaled his own. She cared about him, and soon she would learn to love him. She was his wife in every sense and she was going to remain his wife.

Stalking across the living room, he jerked the front door open. Seeing his business partner didn't take the sting out of Kane's words. "You better have a hell of a good reason for disturbing me."

William Conrad, who had never been the object of the full force of Kane's anger, stepped back. Mouth agape, his cigar teetered precariously between his teeth.

"Spit it out," Kane demanded. "You were anxious enough a moment ago."

"Kane, if you'd stop yelling at the poor man perhaps he could tell you what you want to know."

Kane glanced over his shoulder to see Victoria at the foot of the stairs, her hair softly mussed, her face flushed and beautiful. Her red knit dress clung to every glorious inch of her fantastic body and reminded him of the lacy undergarments he had almost removed before . . . He whirled back to their unwanted guest.

"I'm waiting, William."

Apparently, the reprieve had been enough time for William to regain his composure. "After the decision was made to go into men's skin care you said you wanted to make some changes in the marketing strategy and that you'd get back to me. The press conference is tomorrow to announce the start of Cinnamon II, and I wanted to know all the facts before then."

"Didn't I tell you last week that I needed to check out a few details and I'd get back to you before the press conference?"

"Yes, but—"

"Have I ever lied to you?"

"No, but—"

"Been late with a report?"

"No, but you've never been married before either," William said in a rush.

"I don't think we've been properly introduced." Victoria smiled sweetly as she stepped between the two men. "I'm Victoria Taggart and you must be William Conrad, Kane's partner."

William appeared dazed by the beautiful woman standing before him. It took him a couple of seconds to notice her extended hand. "Hello, Mrs. Taggart. You're lovelier than your picture."

Something that sounded suspiciously like a growl came from Kane. William snatched his hand back.

"Mr. Conrad, you must know that Kane is as dependable as the sunrise," she chided gently. "You can't have worked with him all these years and not learned how trustworthy and responsible he is. If he said he'd have the report to you, he'll have it to you."

The tension eased out of Kane. His wife was defending him again. It was almost worth William's interruption. Almost.

"I suppose," William admitted grudgingly. "My wife calls me a worrier. I like to know where I'm going."

"In other words, you like being in control, and you've found out you can't control Kane," Victoria guessed.

William's startled gaze flew up to Kane.

"I've known you were that way since our first meeting," Kane told him. "But in taking me on as a partner, you showed me you wouldn't put your personal feelings above the company's. You were also willing to work as hard or harder than I was in saving Cinnamon. You didn't sit around crying and feeling sorry for yourself. If you had, I would have walked away even if you had offered me twice the percentage at half the price. I don't have any patience for people who won't help themselves. You were then and you still are, a valuable asset to the company."

Once again, William appeared stunned. "You've never told me this before."

"I don't like explaining myself," Kane told him.

Victoria stared up into her husband's face and

recalled all the times he had patiently explained things to her. She was married to a very special man. He almost made her believe in happily ever after.

William extended his hand, the lines of worry around his eyes gone. "Thanks, Kane. Sorry I disturbed you. It won't happen again."

The older man's hand disappeared into Kane's larger, stronger one. He decided to be as gracious as his partner. "I've already taken care of the changes I wanted, including reserving advertising space in newspapers and magazines for December, talked to a photographer about giving the layout a more outdoor feel, and started searching for another male model who doesn't look as if he hasn't started shaving yet."

"Why didn't . . ." William smiled and shook his graying head. "I almost forgot you don't like explaining yourself. In this case I can guess. Since you left, I've become more demanding. You wanted me to get the message that you won't be pushed."

Kane glanced down into Victoria's upturned face. "Only one person can do that."

"Kane likes for people to trust him," Victoria said.

Once again William's gaze went from Kane to Victoria. "It won't happen again." He went briskly down the steps.

As soon as he got inside his car, Kane closed the front door and picked Victoria up. "I thought I told you to stay put."

Victoria wrapped her arms around his neck and laughed. "You don't sound as if I can make you do anything."

Kane's lips found hers. The kiss was hot, quick and deep. He lifted his head and waited until her eyelids drifted upward. "You make me burn, Tory. You make me fight for control each time I take you in my arms."

Her trembling fingers touched the hard line of his jaw. "You make me feel the same way."

His black eyes blazed. He started for the stairs at a fast clip, carrying her as if she were as weightless as a shadow. The soft outline of her body against his chest proclaimed she was a flesh-and-blood woman. *His* woman. Nudging the bedroom door open with his shoulder, he sat her down and drew her dress over her head in one coordinated movement.

"Don't think I'm easy because I decided to let you have your way with me," she said, and pushed his shirt down his muscular arms.

"If you hadn't, I probably would have kidnapped you." He laid her in the bed, then stripped out of his jeans and undershorts.

With unabashed pride and longing Victoria

stared at Kane's powerful, naked body. He was superb in every breathtaking detail. He had taught her so much, given her so much. She didn't know she could be this happy. "You would have made a magnificent knight."

Kane came down on the bed and gathered her into his arms. "Only if you were the prize."

"Words." Victoria licked the hard brown nub of his nipple and smiled at his groan. "I'd like to see some action."

His hands closed over her lace clad breasts, and when they lifted, the fragile scrap of material was gone. His head bent. "Your wish is my command."

The following days were filled with revelations for Victoria. No longer did she try to analyze her emotions. She reacted on impulse and continued to be rewarded with more happiness than she had experienced in her entire lifetime. To her added pleasure, she quickly discovered, she couldn't have been more wrong in telling Kane she didn't want whispers of sweet nothings. She unashamedly relished every sensual promise he made . . . and its fulfillment. One night after dinner, she told him as much. He smiled like a conquering knight, swept her into his arms and took her to bed. The next day, Bonnie and Clair Benson took credit for the glow in Victoria's face.

Bonnie she teased about no longer being afraid of getting an arrow in her back. Her grandmother she let think what she would. Victoria knew Kane deserved the real credit. At Addie's graduation, she and Kane were never more than a few feet apart. Relatives of Kane's she hadn't met gave Victoria as many hugs and congratulations as they did the graduate.

"I don't think I've ever seen Kane this happy."

Victoria turned to see Matt standing beside her, but his gaze was on Kane taking a picture of Addie in her cap and gown, with their parents. "He might not have been if you hadn't set me stra—"

"Forget it," Matt interrupted, his eyes finally coming back to her. "Just keep him happy."

Victoria frowned at the odd inflection of his voice. "Was that a threat or a command?"

"Both," he said, and walked over to drape an arm around Addie's shoulders.

"What was that all about?"

Startled, Victoria glanced around to see Bonnie. "He's afraid I might hurt Kane. I wouldn't do that."

"I hate to bring this up, but what are you going to do when your time together is up?"

The question was one Victoria had refused to let herself think about. "I don't know, but I'm not going to hurt Kane."

Uneasiness crept into Bonnie's expression. "If you leave, I don't see how you're going to be able to avoid it . . . for either of you."

Chapter 13

Thirteen days. Thirteen days were left of the three months she had agreed to spend with Kane. It seemed rather prophetic that she and Kane had eloped with thirteen days left on the deadline her grandmother had given her. She had known what to do then. She wished she knew what to do now.

At least she wasn't still hung up on her hatred of Stephen. The previous night in Dallas, at a performance by the Black Dance Theatre benefiting the Museum of African-American Life and Culture, she had looked up during intermission and seen her ex-husband. Seeing her, Stephen almost ran from the lobby of the Majestic Theatre.

Instead of rage, she felt sadness that she had wasted so much time hating. She had glanced up at Kane and wanted to be home and in bed with her husband. She whispered her own sensual promise in his ear. Hand in hand they quickly left the theatre.

A secret smile on her face, she leaned back in her chair and looked around her office. For once, it was free of the usual clutter of shipping boxes, lingerie, freestanding racks, mannequins, props, and an odd assortment of other things. Kane had "organized" things for her. She would have gotten around to it before the big summer sale, but he seemed to enjoy helping her.

Men and women customers certainly liked having him around. They weren't bashful about asking his opinion, and with a wicked gleam in his eyes, he had been quick to point out his preference. Sales had soared. Customers had actually been disappointed that morning to learn he wasn't coming in.

Victoria couldn't blame them; she didn't want to think of a day without seeing Kane. Each minute she spent with him, she wanted a hundred more. She was actually looking forward to his college reunion the following weekend. Yet she wasn't so naive to think that the first bloom of passion would last forever. There had better be something to take its place. She smiled to herself. Passion wasn't so bad, for the time being.

* * *

An hour later, Victoria pulled up in front of the ranch house. Grabbing a bag of groceries in one hand and a picnic basket in the other, she went inside. She had two hours before Kane expected her home. She was going to surprise him with a picnic, and herself. Laughing at her own boldness, she set the bags on the counter.

The sound of an automobile pulling up outside had her rushing to the window. At the sight of a red truck, her shoulders sagged in relief. She went back outside.

A middle-aged man climbed out of the pickup and tipped his straw hat off his balding gray head. "Evening, Mrs. Taggart. I'm Nate Hinson."

"Have we met before?"

"Not in person." He smiled at her confusion. "Kane came into my antique shop about eight years ago and we hit it off right away. I've been out here too many times to count with deliveries. One time he showed me a beautiful, hand-carved cradle. Seems it had been handed down through his mother's family, and she insisted, as the oldest, he keep it. Kane showed me a picture of a pretty young woman about two years ago and told me she'd either be the mother of his child or he wouldn't have one."

"Kane showed you a picture and a cradle?"

"That he did," Mr. Hinson repeated. "The re-finishing job on the cradle is one of the best I've ever seen. He put a lot of love into that job. Used to keep it in his workshop covered up and waiting. There's not a person around who isn't happy for him getting married. We sure would have liked to have been there to see it."

Kane had refinished a cradle for another woman. Pain ripped through her. Only years of training kept her upright and helped Victoria to mumble, "I-I'm sorry."

"Don't you go apologizing. We are all fond of that husband of yours. Everyone around knows what a good man he is and how much he loves kids." Mr. Hinson shook his head. "If you need help with a project with kids, just ask Kane."

She pressed her hand against her empty womb. "Yes."

"Nice seeing good things happen to a good man like Kane." Hinson glanced around the well-tended yard and the painted buildings beyond. "This place was going to seed until Kane bought it. That barn had a hole in it as big as my truck, and this house hadn't had a coat of paint on it in years. Good thing it was built to last. Never saw a man so good at turning throwaways into something worthwhile."

Victoria thought of herself: thrown away by Stephen and refurbished by Kane—but she was just a substitute.

"Here I am running on and you probably need to be getting on with supper. I saw this rocker at an estate sale yesterday and thought of Kane and the cradle." Unhooking the tailgate of the truck, he unloaded the high-backed mahogany rocker and set it down on the porch. "When I saw Kane in town a couple of weeks back I asked him if you were the one in the picture and he just grinned. Never seen a man so happy or proud."

Victoria's gaze clung to the rocker. Her throat clogged. Tears stung her eyes.

"It's my wedding gift to you and Kane. I better be going. The way those clouds are rolling in, it looks like we might have a bit of a storm." Closing the tailgate, he got inside the vehicle. "Good day, Mrs. Taggart."

The instant the door closed, Victoria tore down the steps and around the house to Kane's workshed. It took less than a minute for her to locate the small object, covered by the type of protective padding movers use. Her hand trembled as she lifted the cover.

A cradle. Not a speck of dust touched the gleaming mahogany surface.

Tears rolled down her cheeks. Kane might have wanted a substitute wife, but not a substitute mother for his children. He still loved another woman. Agony rolled over her in waves. Somehow, she managed to stand. She had one thought: to leave before Kane came back. It wasn't his fault she had played her part too well. She hadn't realized until that agonizing moment that she had confused passion with love. She loved Kane.

Her fingers clamped and unclamped on the smooth wooden surface of the cradle. Wearily, she turned, took a step, and came to an abrupt halt. Kane filled the doorway.

Pain and misery washed over her. And the one person in the world who she would have run to for consolation was the person who had caused her such pain.

"Honey, come inside and let's talk."

She watched him move closer and lift his hand toward her face. "Don't. Don't touch me."

Anguish ripped through Kane's gut. Having Victoria recoil from him now was worse than anything he had ever experienced. He had met Hinson a mile from the ranch. At the mention of the cradle and rocker, Kane had gunned his truck. It had taken less than five minutes to reach her, but he was too late. Victoria might want his body, but not his baby.

"Things can be as they were before. Forget about the cradle," Kane told her, aware of the pleading note in his voice and unable to do anything about it.

Victoria flinched. She looked at the man she loved. Big, brawny, and gentle, he still had the power to make her knees weak. If she thought there was a chance for him to forget about the other woman, she might stay. But two years and a cradle were too much to fight. She walked past Kane as if he didn't exist.

She knew he followed her inside the house and up the stairs. There was nothing she could do about that now. All her concentration was on getting her car keys and going someplace to nurse her pain in private. She was paying the price for caring, for being vulnerable.

"You're not leaving."

She opened her mouth, felt the sting in her throat and in her eyes. Her hands clamped on the keys. Closing her eyes, she said one word, "Please."

"No. You have thirteen days before the bargain is over and you're not going anyplace," Kane told her.

Her lids lifted. She saw the tortured look on his face, a look she was sure mirrored her own. No matter what, she was sure of one thing: Kane hadn't meant to hurt her. "I can't stay here."

He stepped toward her. "Tory."

"Don't." She bit her lip to keep from crying. "Just let it end."

"You owe me thirteen days, and unless you're

ready to let your grandmother in on why we got married, you're not going anyplace," Kane warned, his voice as expressionless as his face.

"You wouldn't!"

"Try me."

Victoria took one look at his unyielding face and knew he spoke the truth. Kane didn't bluff. "Why do you want me to stay?"

"You haven't stopped running from life. Maybe in the time left you'll learn not to," Kane told her.

Any hope left within her died. Kane didn't want her to stay because he loved her. He was right about one thing—she was too cowardly to stay and see kindness instead of love. "Call her."

Shock rippled across his face. "You don't mean that?"

"I'm leaving."

"You hate me that much?" he said incredulously.

She wanted to shout that she loved him that much, but she couldn't. She was afraid that if she did, she'd fling herself into his arms. At least she'd leave with her pride intact.

Narrowed black eyes studied Victoria's determined face for a long moment. "There's a thunderstorm blowing in. Give me your car keys. I'll drive you."

Kane's voice sounded as bleak as he looked.

Victoria dropped the keys in his outstretched hands. Both of them were at the end of their rope.

Inside the car, she watched the approaching storm and wished the thunder would drown out her thoughts. Kane wanted a woman he couldn't have. She wanted Kane. She bit her lip to keep from crying out or worse, turning to him and asking why he couldn't love her. Blinking back tears, she huddled against the door.

"Dammit, get off that door," Kane snapped as he stopped at a signal light. "I know you don't want me to touch you."

"If only that was true," Victoria whispered, but not softly enough.

"What did you say?" Kane demanded, ignoring a honking horn behind him.

"I want to go home," Victoria said, her voice raw.

"You want! Do you ever think of what someone else wants? Other people get hurt. Other people have dreams. Other people—" He broke off as other motorists made their displeasure known by blasting their car horns. The Jaguar sped through the light on yellow. "I thought you were a woman, not a selfish child who runs when she can't have her way. Maybe it's best you leave."

Victoria shuddered.

"In the morning, I'll have my lawyer draw up the papers for a legal separation. I know you don't want any problems getting a divorce when the year is up. I'll take full responsibility for the marriage failing." He pulled under the covered concrete canopy of her apartment.

She studied the taut lines of his face. "You aren't going to tell my grandmother?"

"What do you think?" he asked impatiently as he got out of the car and opened her door. As soon as she straightened, he held out her keys. When she didn't move, he grabbed her hand and slapped them into her open palm. Without another word, he walked into the driving rain.

Shoulders hunched, head bent, he continued down the street as if impervious to everything. Victoria knew he wasn't. He hurt. So did she. They had hurt each other. All she had to do was go up to her apartment and her life would be as it was before. All her things—Her thoughts came to a shuddering halt.

Even after they started sleeping together, she hadn't taken one household item from her apartment to indicate she wanted to make a life with Kane. How was he supposed to know she wanted to stay with him?

She ran after him. He had given her everything she thought she wanted, but it didn't mean anything if she lost him. She realized that, just as she realized she loved him enough to swallow her pride and make a fool of herself if necessary. She had enough love for both of them. She gasped as the cold, driving ran hit, soaking her within seconds. She ran faster.

"Kane!"

He turned, his voice as thunderous as the skies. "Are you crazy?" He didn't wait for an answer, just picked her up and sprinted back under the protection of the overhang.

Victoria clutched his neck when he started to put her down. "Don't go. I don't care if you *are* in love with that woman you're keeping the cradle for. I'm not giving you a divorce."

"You think I—" Kane broke off abruptly as he noticed that several people who were entering the building had stopped and turned to watch them. He headed inside. Neither appeared concerned with the questioning looks and whispers as they crossed the lobby, rode in the elevator, went down the hallway.

Nor were they concerned that they were soaking wet and dripping water everywhere. As soon as Kane closed her apartment door, he sat her on her feet and barked. "Talk."

Misery welling up inside Victoria, she brushed away the wetness on her face, unsure if it was tears or rain. "The antique dealer told me you showed him a picture of the woman you planned to marry."

"You didn't think to ask me about it," Kane said. "You just assumed and ran."

She sniffed and brushed her hand across her face again. "I couldn't stand to hear about your wanting another woman. But it's better than losing you. You hadn't promised me anything."

"Hadn't I? I remember promising to love, honor and cherish. I remember promising in sickness and in health, until death do us part."

His voice still had a rough edge to it, but the words curled through Victoria like wisps of sunshine lighting all the dark places in her soul, in her heart. "But it was because of the business arrangement."

"Was it? Did you ever think it might not be? Did you ever think that what we had in bed and out of bed was something special?" Hands on his hips, he glared down at her. "I'm tired of you running to me, then away from me. Make up your mind now if you're going to stick with me in good times and in bad."

Tears, this time she was sure, started flowing. "You mean for the next thirteen days?"

"Damn the thirteen days," he shouted. "I'm talking about a lifetime. But you better be sure, because I'm not taking any more of this foolishness from you if you decide to stay. If there's a problem, wc talk it out and we always sleep in the same bed. No sulking and no running away." He glanced around her apartment. "And you get rid of this place."

Anger worked its way past her misery. "You expect me to do all the giving. What about all the talk about us being a team? I may be in love with you, but you're not going to dictate to me."

Kane looked stunned. "You love me?"

"Of course I love you. What do you think I've been trying to tell you? What woman in her right mind wouldn't love someone as handsome and kind and tender as you?"

"Then you have to trust me, Tory. Trust me enough to know I wouldn't sleep with you, make you care about me, if I loved another woman. Listen to your heart. Take this one last step. For me. For you. I promise I won't let you down."

She heard the love in his voice, saw it in his beautiful black eyes, and launched herself into his arms. The one place she had always known solace and comfort. "I love you, Kane. I love you," she repeated through her tears.

He hugged her so hard her ribs hurt. She didn't care, she just held on. "Tory—" His voice broke with emotion. "You did it." He reached for his wallet. "I want to show you something."

Victoria leaned against Kane and waited. Not a shred of apprehension touched her. Love meant trusting and she trusted Kane. He held up a worn and creased black and white newspaper photograph. Her eyes widened. It was a picture of her taken four years earlier, when she had been interviewed about the success of *Lavender and Lace*. Her confused gaze flew up to his.

"I've thought about you off and on since the night of the storm at Bonnie's house. I agreed to help you because I wanted a second chance, to see what might have happened between us. It wasn't until you turned me down at the coliseum that I realized I loved you." His lips brushed against her damp forehead. "I cut your picture out of the newspaper on the pretense of giving it to Bonnie. Instead I tucked it in my wallet. Mr. Hinson saw it when I was paying for a washstand.

"What I told him was more wishful thinking than anything. I had held you once, on a night during a storm like this, and went down for the count. You touched me with your determination to be brave for Bonnie, your love for your grandparents, your innocence. You were beautiful and rich, yet down to earth and strangely insecure. When I picked you up to put you in Bonnie's bed, I didn't want to let you go." He shook his dark head.

"I felt ashamed for wanting you, and you were Bonnie's friend. I tried to forget you, but you'd pop into my head at the strangest times. After your divorce, Bonnie told me you were down on men, so I let it go. At her wedding, I saw you give more than one guy the cold shoulder, so I didn't think I'd do any better. I dated, but it never seemed the right combination. After we kissed that day in the truck, I had to find out if you were the one woman for me."

"What is the right combination?" Victoria asked breathlessly.

Only after his mouth took hers in a deep, searing kiss did he answer her. "Love. Commitment. Trust. Fire."

Her trembling hand touched his lips. "Love. Commitment. Trust. Fire," she repeated solemnly. Tears pricked her eyes again. This time they were tears of joy. "It may sound selfish, but I'm glad another woman wasn't smart enough to make you love her."

"That couldn't happen. I'm yours for a lifetime. I was so scared I couldn't get you to care." His lips grazed against her palm. She shivered. "Your loving me was something I didn't dare let myself dream of."

"I love you with all my heart. Now that you

have me, what are you going to do with me?" she asked as she looked up through a dark sweep of lashes.

He smiled devilishly. "First, we're getting you out of these wet clothes." Scooping her up in his powerful arms, he headed for the bedroom.

"What about you?" she asked as he put her down. "I don't have anything for you to put on."

"Neither one of us will be needing clothes for a long time." He began unbuttoning her dress. He paused on seeing the black lace merrywidow. His questioning gaze met hers.

"I had planned on taking you up the hill for a picnic, then making you an offer you couldn't refuse," she said, her hands busy undoing the buttons on his shirt.

With impatience, Kane finished first. The soggy dress plopped around her feet. She stood before him with the garter straps of the merrywidow taut over a black G-string bikini and the lace hem of black stockings. Kane sucked in his breath. "You're the most beautiful woman I've ever seen."

Her lips grazed his chest. "You make me feel beautiful."

"You make me feel beautiful too," he said without thought.

Victoria raised her head. Her eyes shone with

love and wonder. "I'll never doubt you again. I love you, Kane Taggart."

"I love you, Victoria Taggart."

"Then give me something I want."

"Anything."

The zipper rasped on his jeans. "Give me your baby."

Epilogue

"Kane, come to bed."

"In a minute."

Since over the last two months Victoria had learned that Kane's "minute" could easily turn into an hour, she walked farther into the connecting bedroom.

"I still can't believe they're ours," Kane whispered in awe, his gaze switching back and forth between the two black-haired babies asleep in the spindle cribs.

Victoria smiled and leaned into Kane's hard body, felt his arm curve around her waist. "They're so sweet, the hospital staff probably can't either. I shudder to think what my grandparents and your parents put them through."

"I probably wasn't much better. I've never been so scared in all my life."

"Except when we repeated our vows at church," she reminded him. "You weren't much better at the private reception we had at my grandparents' house."

"That's because you waited until that morning to tell me you were pregnant. I didn't know whether to shout for joy or put you to bed and forbid you to move," he said, defending himself.

Victoria's smile broadened. Kane was still bossy. His fraternity brothers at his college reunion had teased her about being married to such an opinionated man. "If I didn't know how much you love me, I might be jealous of Chandler and Kane junior. The moment the sonogram confirmed twins, you and Mr. Hinson started searching for another cradle. Not that they ever get to be in them, except downstairs, because you think it's too drafty for them."

"A man's got to take care of his family." He pulled her closer.

"We couldn't ask for better." She turned in his arms. "Thank you for not giving up on me. Most of all, thank you for awakening me to love."

"You're my own Sleeping Beauty. I told you I wasn't afraid of a few thorns."

"So you did." Victoria smiled. "But unlike the

fairy tale, the thorns around me didn't turn into beautiful flowers."

"No, like you, they turned into something much better, hidden treasures." His compelling black eyes blazed, his voice dropped to a velvet drawl. "How about we go to bed and thank each other?"

"All right. And this time I'll pretend I don't hear you scream," Victoria said, her eyes alight with amusement as she turned and ran for the bed. Grinning, Kane was right behind her.

Read on for an excerpt from the upcoming book by
Francis Ray

IT HAD TO BE YOU

Coming soon from St. Martin's Paperbacks

She haunted him.

There were times when he could think of nothing else. She was passionate one moment, spurning him the next. She drew him, excited him.

And he couldn't have her.

In his home office in the hills outside of Los Angeles, Zachary Albright Wilder paced the length of the spacious hickory-paneled room, his anger growing with each agitated step. "What do you mean she won't work with me?" Zachary snapped. "Deliver me from divas."

"Now, Rolling Deep," Oscar Winters, his agent, soothed, using Zach's professional nickname. "Forget this one and move on. After two weeks of not taking my phone calls, I was finally able to corner Laurel Raineau's agent and pull from the sharp-tongued woman that it's your reputation with women and for hard partying that has Raineau backing off. Her agent said that your image isn't the kind she wants associated with her classical music."

"What!" Zachary came to a complete stop and shoved his hand through thick, straight black hair that brushed the collar of his shirt. "We're in the twenty-first century for goodness' sake! Sure, I go out with a lot of women, but I'd be suicidal if I was intimate with all of them. I couldn't possibly party as much as the media says or I wouldn't have a wall full of platinum and gold records I've produced."

"Just what I told her agent," Oscar agreed.

"It's not my fault the media chooses to go with what titillates and sells more magazines and newspapers and boosts readership or ratings on the radio or on TV rather than the truth," he said, moving across the handwoven silk rug in front of his massive cherry desk. "To have them tell it, I've slept with every female artist I've ever produced, and in my spare time, there are the movie starlets and heiresses."

"I tried to tell her agent it was all hype, R.D."

R.D., Rolling Deep, was the moniker given to him by one of the first clients he'd ever worked with, a hard-core hip-hop artist whose hero was

Scarface. The name stuck as Zach worked with more and more musicians who came from the street or who wanted people to believe they had.

"Perhaps it's the name." He rubbed the back of his neck. He hadn't thought about it much. To him, the nickname simply meant he didn't have to look to anyone to cover his back. However, he was certain no one feared him. It was the exact opposite. When he went out, he was usually swarmed by autograph seekers or approached by hopeful musicians. He'd changed his cell phone number again just last week because of so many unwanted calls. Twenty-four-hour manned security at the gated entrance of his home wasn't ego, but necessary to maintain his privacy.

"But your name is known all over the world. You have the golden, or should I say, the platinum touch." Oscar chuckled.

"It seems Laurel Raineau didn't get the memo," he said sarcastically. He'd promised himself long ago that he'd never let his success go to his head. He'd seen it wreak havoc with too many lives. Your star could fall even faster than it rose.

"Forget her," Oscar said again. "In two months, you go back into the studio with Satin to do her next album. She was at Spargo last night and asked about you."

Zach grunted. The restaurant in L.A. was one

of "the" places to be seen. The very reason Zach seldom went there anymore. Satin had the voice of an angel and the sexual appetite of a succubus. While working with her on her last album, he'd flatly told her that if she didn't stop coming on to him, he was walking. He had never been intimate with a client and he didn't intend to be.

He should just move on as Oscar said, but he couldn't. Despite her snobbish attitude, when Laurel Raineau picked up a violin, it was pure magic. The music drew you, moved you. Passion and fire.

Laurel was five-feet-three and probably weighed one hundred and ten pounds soaking wet with all of her clothes on. Yet, her music was more powerful than any he had ever heard, and he'd listened to and played musical instruments for as long as he could remember.

For personal and professional reasons he wanted to produce her next album. As a free agent, he was in a position to pick and choose his projects. There was a long list of musical entertainers from every genre who wanted to work with him.

All except Laurel Raineau. That stopped today. "Did you get her address?"

"I did," Oscar answered, relief in his voice that he had been able to do at least one thing his biggest client had asked. "It's a couple of miles from you, actually." He gave him the address.

Zach was moving behind his desk before his agent finished. "Hold." He pressed the intercom to the garage. "Toby, bring the car around immediately."

"Be right there, Zach."

Toby Yates, friend, former drag car racer, and chauffeur was one of the few people who called Zachary by his name. "Talk to you later, Oscar."

"If you took no for an answer, you wouldn't be where you are today. Bye."

Zachary disconnected the call and headed for the front door. Ms. Snob wouldn't find it so easy to ignore him. She'd have to tell him to his face all the crap she'd said about him—if she had the courage.

Opening the twelve-foot door, Zachary quickly went down the fourteen steps to the waiting black Bentley. Toby was there with the back door open as Zach had known he'd be.

"Thanks." Zachary practically dove inside. He didn't need a chauffeur most of the time, but there were occasions when he was working on a song, was too tired after seemingly endless hours in the recording studio, or with a client that he didn't want to drive. It also gave Toby a reason to stick to his sobriety. He'd been with Zach ever since Zach had come to L.A. against his father's wishes to make a name for himself in the music industry.

Zach's fist clenched. He'd done what he'd set out to do, but the rift between him and his father had never mended before his death.

The car pulled off smoothly and started down the long drive. The iron gates swung open. He gave Toby the address, but he wouldn't need a GPS system. He'd grown up in L.A. and knew the streets well.

In a matter of minutes, Toby turned up a steep hill that gradually leveled off. Up ahead was the ambiguous iron gate. Zach felt a muscle leap in his jaw. Toby pulled up until the back window of the car was even with the speaker box.

Zach rolled down the window and punched the black button. "Zachary Wilder to see Ms. Raineau."

"Ms. Raineau is unavailable."

Zachary held on to his temper. It wouldn't do any good to blow. The person was just following orders. "Perhaps if you'd tell her who is calling, she might change her mind."

"The answer would be the same," came the droll answer.

Patience. "If you would please just tell her."

"Sir. She is unavailable and this conversation is over."

Zachary locked the curse behind his lips. If he ever got his hands on Ms. Snob, he'd have a few choice words with her. He sat back in his seat. "Home."

Toby pulled off and started back down the road. Arms folded, Zachary slumped back in his seat. Somehow, some way, he was going to talk to her.

"Zach, a stretch limo just came out of the gate."

Zach shot up in his seat. Sure enough, there was a black limo behind them. The car could have dropped her off or anyone else off or have someone else inside. "Once we're on the street, follow it and don't let it get away."

Toby snorted, straightened his mirror. "You're such a kidder."

Zach grinned. Toby lived for speed. He might not have a GPS system, but he did have the latest radar detector.

The limo passed, and although Zach already knew he wouldn't be able to see inside, he leaned closer to the window. "Can you tell if it's a car service or private?"

"Service," Toby answered.

The chances went up that Laurel might be in the car. People who were as successful as she usually had a personal driver. They tended to be more loyal and they were on hand whenever you needed them, but Laurel hadn't been in L.A. long enough to hire a driver.

"He's taking the exit to LAX."

Better and better. Zachary watched the limo take the lane for departing international flights. "Ten bucks says Ms. Snob is in that car."

"Not this time," Toby said good-naturedly. "I always lose when I bet with you."

Laughing, sensing he'd run Laurel to ground at last, Zach scooted forward in the back seat. "I've got you now."

"The paparazzi are always hanging out here. You're going to have to be fast on your feet to get past them," Toby warned.

Zach had always been courteous in the past. It was better that way. However, today he had no intention of letting the horde with cameras and mics slow him down.

The limo inched its way over to the curb and parked. Toby muscled the Bentley in ahead of a Jaguar. The man in the car laid on his horn in protest. "You better hurry. I'll circle."

Zach was already reaching for the door handle. On the sidewalk, he hurried toward baggage check-in for first-class passengers. He didn't see her at first, until a guy who looked like he could bench-press five hundred pounds and not break a sweat moved to reveal a delicately shaped woman wearing large-rimmed sunglasses, a short-brimmed woven hat edged with black ribbon, a white blouse, and slim black pants. On the other side of her was a twin to the first guy.

Laurel Raineau. Victory. Grinning, Zach moved to follow her into the terminal. He made it within five feet of her before one of the twin samurai faced him, blocking his way. He moved to step around him. The man moved with him.

"You're in my way," Zachary said.

The man said nothing.

Zachary tried to look past or over him, but that was impossible. He was a yard wide. "Should I call airport security?"

The bodyguard folded his massive arms.

"Rolling Deep!" a female voice screeched. "It's Rolling Deep!" The cry was taken up by another and another. If he had miraculously managed to escape the attention of the paparazzi earlier, he was in for it now.

A crowd converged on him. Cameras flashed. The bodyguard moved back, then turned and walked away. There was no way Zach would try to follow. People would follow him. If he got close to her again, her bodyguards would stop him. He was sure security was nearby, watching to see that things remained relatively calm.

All he needed was Laurel seeing him having an altercation with the authorities. She already thought the worst of him. Swallowing his disappointment, he signed any paper and legal body parts presented to him.

Laurel had managed to escape him.